SEALS

"You will move out onto the platform and kneel," said the terrorist leader.

Pruit hesitated. He knew what was coming. A bullet in the back of the head. They were going to shoot him in the back of the head just as sure as the plane was sitting in the desert. They were going to dump his body on the tarmac so that the news minicams could photograph him lying there, the juices baking from him as his blood seeped onto the concrete, staining it crimson.

His training in the Navy had told him exactly what to do. Instructors had screamed at him, "What do you do if surrounded by five hundred enemy soldiers?"

The answer was simple: "Kill them."

He felt the prod of a pistol in the small of his back. That was the mistake the amateur made . . .

ATTACK!

SEALS
#11

ATTACK!

STEVE MACKENZIE

AVON BOOKS ◆ NEW YORK

SEALS #11: ATTACK! is an original publication of Avon Books. This work has never before appeared in book form. This work is a novel. Any similarity to actual persons or events is purely coincidental.

AVON BOOKS
A division of
The Hearst Corporation
105 Madison Avenue
New York, New York 10016

Copyright © 1989 by Kevin D. Randle
Published by arrangement with the author
Library of Congress Catalog Card Number: 88-92107
ISBN: 0-380-75582-3

First Avon Books Printing: January 1989

AVON TRADEMARK REG. U.S. PAT. OFF. IN IN OTHER COUNTRIES, MARCA REGISTRADA, HECHO EN U.S.A.

Printed in the U.S.A.

K–R 10 9 8 7 6 5 4 3 2 1

For Bruce W. Platt,
who was there when I needed him
and who always seems to have the right answer.
Thanks.
—K.D.R.

ATTACK!

1

It was supposed to be a vacation. A trip from his station in Italy, into the Middle East, and then into India, land of Rudyard Kipling and the Bengal Lancers. A sightseeing tour into an area that he'd read about since his boyhood, and thanks to the United States Navy, a place that he was going to get to visit for very little money.

Allen Pruit had not been concerned about the landing for passengers in Athens, Greece. He knew that airport security there was terrible, but then it wasn't much better in Rome, where he'd boarded the flight. In one airport they let the terrorists onto the airplanes, and in the other they kept them off the plane and in the airport terminal, machine-gunning only a relatively few passengers.

But those things were rare and it was bad luck when the path of the passengers crossed that of terrorists. The same could be said of the people who were killed by lightning and snake bite and man-eating tigers. There was nothing you could do to protect yourself from the random bad luck that could kill—except lock yourself in your room, and then the damn thing would probably catch on fire.

No, Pruit wasn't one of those who let the possible stop him from having fun. If terrorists took over the plane, it would be one more interesting thing to happen. They rarely killed anyone, preferring to sit for days on a runway while the news media of the entire world provided them with a forum for their ridiculous and one-sided views.

The jet left the runway in Athens, climbed into a bright blue sky and passed over the deep azure of the sea below them. Puffy white clouds dotted the scene outside the aircraft. Pruit was happy with life and the way things were going. The Navy recruiter who'd talked about fun, travel and adventure hadn't been far off. And to make it better, Pruit was stationed in Europe, while many of his fellows were stationed in Southeast Asia, dodging mortars and bullets and enemy attacks.

The captain had just turned off the seatbelt sign when two men, dressed in khaki, their faces hidden by kaffiyeh, left their seats. One of them headed toward the rear of the plane where the restrooms were located. The other pushed through the curtain that separated the first-class section from the rear. Pruit looked up to see that and then returned his gaze to the window, where he was trying to spot ships on the Mediterranean Sea.

The piercing scream caught him by surprise. He jumped and turned in time to see the man, his face still hidden, jam a pistol against the head of the blond stewardess. Another woman screamed and three men were shouting. One man stood up, moving toward the aisle.

The gunman swung his pistol around, pointed it right at the face of the man standing, who raised his hands slowly and then dropped back into his seat. His eyes were on the floor so that he couldn't see what was going on.

The second man, who had disappeared into the first-class cabin, pushed back through the curtain, a pistol on a brunette. There was a bruise on the side of her face and she was crying.

"You people, stay," he shouted in English. He repeated the order in Arabic and his partner shouted in French.

There was shouting everywhere. People screaming questions, yelling instructions, trying to shut one another up. One man stood up in the aisle, his fists clenched. He looked like he was about to attack. The terrorists saw him and the one holding the brunette aimed over the shoulder of his partner. The man froze but didn't sit down.

"We command this aircraft," said the leader. "You do as told and you will not be hurt."

The woman sitting next to Pruit leaned close to him and said, "My God, I'm Jewish."

"Don't worry," said Pruit. "They'll be more interested in the Americans."

As he said it, he realized that they would be more interested in him than the other Americans. As dictated by regulations, he carried his military ID card, which identified him as an NCO in the Navy. And to make it worse, he had an official passport. It meant only that he'd gotten it through official military channels, but the terrorists wouldn't know that, even if they knew the difference between the civilian passport and the government one.

Almost as if they had read his mind, the leader shouted, "You will all hand in your passports."

No one moved. They sat stunned, watching the terrorists with wide eyes. A few of the women were crying, as were some of the children.

Pruit pulled his passport from his pocket and as he did, shoved his military ID down in the crack of the seat. The passport told the terrorists enough about him. He didn't want the ID card to tell them the rest.

The blond stewardess was pushed in the middle of the back and the terrorist leader ordered, "You pick up passports. You bring them to me."

As the stewardess moved along the aisle collecting the passports, Pruit looked out the window, at the tranquil sea far below him. There was an aircraft carrier, surrounded by the screening ships and the support vessels cruising slowly. The American Navy making a show of force in the eastern end of the Mediterranean Sea. He could see them easily and was sure there were men on the ships looking up at him. All the help he could use and yet there was nothing that those men could do to help him.

The stewardess finished her rounds, carrying the huge stack of passports forward, toward the terrorists. She dropped one, stooped to pick it up and dropped three more. She fell to her knees, her small hands trying to hold most of the documents to her chest while she struggled to pick up those she had dropped. She was crying, the tears staining her cheeks.

Pruit wanted to lean forward and tell her to relax. Tell her that the terrorists were after power and wouldn't hurt anyone if everyone cooperated. But to do that would call attention to himself and that also was something that shouldn't be done. Remain quiet and anonymous. That was the secret to survival in a hijacking situation. Remain anonymous.

The lead hijacker disappeared through the curtain again and there was shouting in the first-class area. Someone was demanding to be let go because he didn't belong there. The shouting was ended by a punch and a groan.

A moment later, the captain came on the intercom. "Ladies and gentlemen, it seems that we have been diverted from our original destination to Libya. Please do not worry. I have been promised that no one will be hurt."

Pruit understood that. He'd been through training in connection with his Navy job that told him the same thing. Hijackers, if they weren't in the mold of D.B. Cooper who did it for money, wanted publicity for their cause. Killing the hostages reduced the sympathy for that cause and, in fact, inflamed people against it.

"I've never been to Libya," he whispered to his seatmate. Now he noticed her for the first time. A young woman who had slipped into her seat, kept her nose buried in a book as Pruit had stared out the window and hadn't invited any conversation.

"I don't want to go," she said, her voice low, but calmer than it had been.

"A little discomfort, a little tension, and the ordeal will be over in a couple of hours."

"I hope you're right," she said, touching his hand.

"I am," he responded, but he wasn't sure about it. These hijackers didn't have the same confident air that most did and that worried him.

Navy Lieutenant Mark Tynan lay on top of the sheets, the overhead fan blowing down on him and closed his eyes. The room was dark because the shades were pulled. If he looked, he could see sunlight blazing around the cracks at the sides of the blinds. Heat seemed to radiate from the windows and the air conditioner struggled to keep up with it.

Tynan was a young man, tall and slim. He had short, light brown hair and light blue eyes. Although a graduate of the University of Colorado, he spent little time in the state now that he was in the Navy. He had thin, sharp features and deeply tanned skin, the result of several months in tropic environments from Southeast Asia to South America to Africa.

He rolled over, put his hands under his chin and looked at the bathroom door. It opened slowly and Stephanie King stood there, naked. A young woman with long, light-colored hair, she held a Ph.D. in cultural anthropology. Like Tynan, she was slim. Her face was angular and her features were fine. From the side, her chin looked to be pointed, but when she turned to face him, it softened slightly. She leaned against the door and asked, "Don't you ever get tired?"

"No," he said. "Not ever. You get tired and the next thing you know, you've slept away your life."

She left the bathroom and walked slowly toward the TV that was set on the combination night stand/dresser/desk of the hotel room. She crouched in front of it and turned it on, waiting for the picture to appear and the sound to come up so that she could adjust it.

Tynan studied her back as she crouched. He watched the muscles bunch, flex and relax and thought that she had a beautiful back, unmarked by anything except the hint of a line where the top of her swimming suit fastened and blocked the tanning rays of the sun.

"You want the news or cartoons?" she asked.

"News," said Tynan. "Cartoons are too violent for me."

"Sure," she said. She flipped the channels until she found an intense young man staring into the camera. She turned up the sound then moved to the bed. Backing up, she sat on the edge of it.

Tynan slipped around so that his feet were near the pillows. With his knuckles he rubbed her spine, watching her shiver as he touched her. Finally he reached around her.

"Hey, I thought you wanted to watch the news."

Tynan glanced at the young man and said, "He's not my type. Too pretty."

"You'd better watch what you're saying," she warned. "Someone might take offense."

"You don't have to worry," he said, grinning broadly. "You're not too pretty."

She turned to face him. "I'm not sure that I like that."

"Well," he said, drawing out the words, "there are ways to obtain a re-evaluation. I might point out that the judge can be bribed."

"I have no money," she said innocently, gesturing at her naked body.

"Money is of little value to me. I'm sure that you can think of something."

But before she could think of something, the intense young man on the television caught Tynan's attention. He shifted around so that he sat next to King, as naked as she. He wanted to watch the report.

A picture of a Boeing 707 came up and then a picture of the Athens Airport, followed by a map of the Mediterranean Sea and a bright explosion near the capital of Libya.

"Damn," said Tynan.

"You know someone on that flight?"

Tynan glanced at her and shook his head. "No. There shouldn't be anyone on it I know. I just . . . it's the cowardice of the hijackers. They'll take on a group of unarmed civilians but you don't see them trying anything where the opposition has an equal chance."

He stopped talking and listened as the newsman told him about the hijackers' demands for a homeland, freedom for brothers in foreign jails and worldwide recognition of their cause.

"News media's a big help too. Grab a jet and your face and your demands become worldwide news."

King looked at the screen, but now the news had changed again. The war in Vietnam was being discussed. Students were protesting in the streets and Jane Fonda was doing everything she could think of to give aid and comfort to the enemy. She couldn't seem to comprehend that time spent in Hanoi would inspire the North Vietnamese to kill more Americans.

Tynan was interested in that too. The media and the protestors had lost sight of the real problem. He could talk until his voice was gone and his words barely audible, but all those in the streets and all those reporting on it didn't understand that the enemy wanted to hear all about the protests and the opposition to American involvement in Southeast Asia. It kept their morale up while undercutting that of the Americans.

He got up and slapped a hand against the TV, turning it off. He glanced at King, who had retreated to the pillow and lay propped there for him to admire.

Forgetting about the protestors and the hijackers and the situation in the world, he said, "You can either cover yourself so that we can order breakfast, or stay like that and see what develops."

For a moment she considered the proposition and then grinning slowly pulled up the sheet so that she was covered from the neck down. "Food," she said.

Tynan laughed. "That's what I get. Now, I suppose that not only do I have to make the call for room service, but you're going to make me pay for it."

"You're the one with the high-paying Navy job. I'm just a poor college teacher."

"Seems to me," said Tynan, "you make as much, or even more, money than I and no one is shooting at you."

"You offered food and now you have to buy it for me. It's your own fault."

Tynan took a deep breath and exhaled slowly. He walked to the window and looked out on the city baking under an already harsh sun. Golden brown desert that stretched to brown mountains surrounded them. The heat was rising from the tops of the buildings, shimmering patterns that told him it was hot out there.

He let the blinds fall shut and turned to the phone. "You know what you want?"

"Sure. Eggs, fried, or rather basted, toast, orange juice and some pancakes."

"Good God. That's going to take a month's pay. Room service isn't cheap."

"Well," she said, "it's better than a poke in the eye with a sharp stick."

He picked up the phone, dialed room service and then glanced at the blank screen of the TV, wondering what was happening in the hijacking.

Although there had been no physical abuse of the passengers in the plane, the terrorists had made them all move. First all the women and children were herded to the rear, then the older men. Pruit was in a group of young men, the military-age men who were put in the front rows in a cabin where they could be more easily watched. That finished, the terrorists separated out the Americans and moved them into the first-class cabin.

Again, Pruit wasn't *worried*. Concerned because this was something that wasn't normal in hijacking. Logical, but not normal. Pruit sat near another window, watching both the scene outside the aircraft and the one unfolding in front of him in the cabin.

The terrified stewardess stood near the door that led into the cockpit and cried. The leader stood with one hand on her shoulder and his head stuck into the doorway. He was giving orders to the flight crew, but Pruit couldn't hear them.

For two hours they all sat quietly. The terrorists—Pruit now learned that there were four of them, including a woman wearing a silk dress that looked expensive—roamed the aisle of the plane, shouting at the passengers. They made demands, stole watches and jewelry and threatened to shoot people who didn't respond fast enough.

Finally, after it seemed that the ordeal would never end, they landed, taxied across the nearly deserted airfield and stopped near a huge chainlink fence that opened onto a desert that stretched as far as Pruit could see. The engines were shut down and the air conditioning was turned off. In moments the fuselage of the jet began to bake.

As it got hotter in the plane, tempers began to flare. There was shouting in the rear. A man's voice demanding that he be allowed to leave. Then a woman saying that she needed to go to the restroom. And suddenly it seemed that everyone in the rear of the aircraft was shouting.

The terrorist leader walked into the rear, stood there and then fired a single round through the top of the fuselage. As soon as he pulled the trigger, the plane fell silent. He shouted orders and then returned to the front.

Outside, Pruit saw several military trucks pull up and

surround the aircraft. At first he believed that it was the local military establishing a cordon around the plane, but then three men approached. One terrorist moved to the front, opened the door and waited. A moving ramp was pushed into place and the three men climbed it, entering the aircraft.

The leader of the terrorists embraced the leader of the military. They talked in low tones, laughing frequently. The terrorist showed the military man the passports and then pointed at the group confined in the first-class cabin. He looked pointedly at Pruit. Pruit didn't return the gaze and didn't make eye contact. He wanted to be ignored by the terrorists.

The whole group moved from the first-class area into the rear of the plane. One man guarded those up front. A young man with wide, frightened eyes. Pruit studied him carefully, cautiously and secretly. He knew that he could take the man easily. But then he'd have to run from the aircraft, past the armed soldiers and into a hostile environment. If he could get out of the plane, there was no place to escape to.

A few minutes later, the terrorists and the military men returned. They stood near the door to the cockpit and were holding only three passports. The terrorist looked at the men sitting in the first-class section, shifted through the passports and then said, "Who is Allen Pruit?"

In that moment, Pruit knew it wasn't going to be a normal hijacking. He knew that he'd have to be very careful if he planned on surviving it.

2

By the middle of the day, Tynan knew that the hijacking he'd heard about in the Middle East was going to be different from those that had gone on before. He had seen enough of the news reports, heard enough of the bulletins to know that the hijackers were serious terrorists who wouldn't hesitate to kill if that fit their purpose. Though the news media and the officials in Libya didn't seem to understand that, Tynan knew it from the way the terrorists were portrayed on the news. He could tell by the way they kept their faces covered, even in the sweltering heat of the Libyan desert, and by the way they refused to let the women or even the children go. They were ruthless men who were making all kinds of demands and all the governments were running around, unsure of what to do.

After he had finished breakfast, taken a shower and dressed, he had thought about calling Washington and offering his assistance to them. He'd been involved in a number of strange missions, some of them for the State Department, and he knew who to call. He could give them advice, but then decided not to bother. They knew where he was, and if they felt the need for his help, they would call him.

Instead, he took the elevator down to the casino and walked into it, where he could watch the people playing the slot machines. Already there were dozens of people there, some of them at the nickel slots, pumping coins into them as fast as they could. Close to them were more people plugging change into the quarter slots and not far away were the dollar slots with the promise of million-dollar payoffs.

He walked down a series of short steps and watched as several people played blackjack. He watched as the dealer flipped over the cards and then showed her own hand. She took a two of diamonds, was under sixteen, and took another card. With sixteen showing, house rules dictated that she take still another card. When she turned up the five, giving her twenty-one, she raked in all the chips.

One man stood up and said, "Shit! How come they always get the cards?" He stomped off, found another table and sat down there.

Tynan wandered around the casino, surprised that everyone smoked. There were no clocks and the doors were made of smoked glass, making it impossible to tell the time of day. The people gambling were wearing a variety of clothes from dressy evening wear to rumpled casual attire.

A woman wearing a coin changer moved toward Tynan and he got a roll of quarters. He moved to the slot machines, studied the front of several of them and then opened his roll. If he played five quarters at once, there were five ways to win and the pots were larger. If he played one quarter, there was only one way to win and the jackpots were much smaller.

"What the hell?" he asked the machine. He plugged in five quarters, pulled the handle and waited as the dials spun. The cherries paid him four quarters.

He smiled at that. The machine told him the winner had been paid, but at that rate, he would eventually run out of money. Winning four for every five he bet was no way to get rich.

He pulled a stool over, sat down and tried again. This

time he won nothing. The wheels stopped spinning and, although there were five ways to win, he hadn't found one of them.

Next to him an older woman sat down. She held a plastic cup from the casino across the street. She dumped her quarters into the tray at the base of the slot machine. That done, she lit a cigarette and began shoving quarters into the machine as quickly as she could. Once she glanced at Tynan, smiled and went back to work.

Tynan was moving slowly, trying to make his money last as long as possible. The woman was feeding it in as quickly as she could, irritated by the tiny jackpots that paid her ten or twenty coins. She wanted to win the big one.

It was amazing to Tynan. He'd seen the signs outside the casinos that said they paid off 97.5 percent of the time. People didn't realize that it meant you would win nine dollars and seventy-five cents for every ten dollars you put into the machines.

Still, there were those who won four or five hundred dollars, a few who won a thousand or two and the very rare individual who picked up a couple of hundred thousand. That was what kept the people stuffing money into the slots. That once-in-a-lifetime shot at making a great deal of money in a few seconds for a tiny investment.

He'd worked his way through most of his roll of quarters, won a few small jackpots that kept him going, when King appeared behind him.

"That's not the way to make money," she said.

"You're an expert on gambling?"

"No, but I am a cultural anthropologist and I understand what makes people do this."

"So how do I beat the system?" he asked.

"Don't gamble. All the odds are with the house. Use the facilities, eat the cheap food and walk through the casinos without spending a cent."

Tynan fed five quarters into the machine and pulled the handle. He got two in return.

"See," she said. "You're not going to win."

The woman whirled and snapped, "If you're not interested in gambling, what the hell are you doing here?"

"I'm—"

"Why don't you keep your stupid theories to yourself," said the woman. She turned back to her machine.

"There you have it," said Tynan, feeding in another five quarters. He got nothing in return.

King shook her head and asked, "What's the fun in that?"

"Hell," said Tynan, "I just might win the four thousand quarters and, if not, I might win a hundred or two hundred or five hundred."

"Well, you'd better do it fast," said King. "You got a call a few minutes ago. Said they'd call you back in thirty minutes."

Tynan looked up and said, "How much longer we got?"

"About fifteen minutes. Just enough time to walk through the casino and catch the elevator back up to the room."

"Hell," said Tynan. "I knew I should have lied to them and not told them where I'd be, but I was sure they could survive without me for a couple of days."

For a moment after the terrorist had called his name, Pruit sat there quietly. He was aware that the others were looking around, trying to spot the unfortunate Pruit. Finally he said, quietly, "I'm Pruit."

"You are an American official."

"Not really," said Pruit. "I received my passport through official channels."

"You are official," said the terrorist again.

Pruit didn't respond to that. There was nothing that he could say to convince them that he wasn't some type of official and if he explained that he was in the Navy, it would probably make the situation worse.

"You come forward. We have demands."

Pruit stood and worked his way to the aisle. He walked to the front of the cabin and said, again, "I have no official power at all."

"The Americans will not allow one of their officials to be injured. They will listen."

"I'm afraid that you don't understand the situation at all," said Pruit. "I'm of no importance to them. They'll have a hard time learning my identity and when they do, it'll do nothing for you."

The leader grinned at Pruit and said, "They will listen to protect one of their own." Then, as if to underscore his point, he slapped Pruit on the side of the head with his pistol. Pain flared and flashed and Pruit fell to his knees. Blood splattered and then dripped. Pruit clapped his hands to the side of his head, but made no sound.

"Our demands are simple. If they are not accepted, then we will kill passengers. You will be the first. Your government will have to apply pressure on their Israeli friends if you are to survive the night."

Slowly Pruit got to his feet. He dropped his hands to his side and said, "My government will not listen. You can shoot me and they will not listen. You can shoot us all and they will not listen."

"You better hope that they place a higher value on your life than you do."

Pruit stood there staring at the man. There was nothing that he could say that would change his mind. The terrorist was convinced that Pruit had some value to the U.S. government. He was convinced that the U.S. government would not allow Pruit to be killed. It was an optimistic view because Pruit knew that it wasn't true.

"You may sit down while we negotiate with the various officials here."

Pruit returned to his seat. He wanted to touch his wound, probe it, but didn't want to give the terrorists the satisfaction of knowing they had hurt him. He pretended to be unaware of the wound.

As he sat there, watching the men move about the cabin, the desert heat blowing in the open door, he realized that this wasn't a typical hijacking. Obviously the hijackers had the support of the Libyan government. The plane hadn't been surrounded by Libyan troops to keep the situation isolated and the hijackers confined, but to help the hijackers keep the passengers corraled. There would be no people slipping off into the night as had happened in the past.

Although he wanted to look outside, he refrained. He knew what he would see. A dozen vehicles, personnel carriers, jeeps with machine guns mounted in the rear, and probably a couple of staff cars that were air conditioned. They'd have to be air conditioned because it was too hot for them not to be. The temperature in the plane was already well over a hundred. Pruit was sweating heavily, his shirt soaked down the back, front and under the arms.

There was no breeze either. The air was stagnant as the jet liner cooked. Although the white paint on the outside reflected some of the heat, it didn't reflect enough. There were passengers sitting there who looked as if they were about to pass out. And if it was that bad up front where the young, healthy males were, then in the rear with the women, children and elderly, it had to be worse.

The terrorists, and their military assistants, left the airplane repeatedly, so that they could cool off. They passed canteens and wine bladders around, drinking from them but offering none of the relief to their captives.

The time passed slowly. Pruit spent it thinking about swimming pools, cold beers and bikini clad women who would all have a crush on him. He tried to ignore the heat that radiated through the thin metal of the fuselage, although he now believed he knew what a baked potato felt like. He might never eat another baked potato.

The terrorist leader entered the plane finally, having been gone for a long time. He moved toward Pruit and said, "There has been no progress in the talks. The governmental officials do not seem to believe that we mean business."

Pruit didn't say a word.

"A demonstration of force is necessary. We must convince the officials that we mean business. I'm afraid that it is bad news for you. Stand up."

The last two words were barked out. An order. Pruit got to his feet and moved up the aisle. He stopped at the door to the cockpit and looked inside. Both pilots sat there, the headphones on the console between them. Their white shirts were as wet as if they had just been taken from the washer, the fabric clinging to their skin. Neither of them looked back, out of the cockpit and into the passenger cabin.

Pruit was pushed toward the door that lead to the outside. In the bright sun reflecting from the sand beyond the chain link fence, he saw a line of tanks. He thought they were Soviet made PT-76s, but wasn't sure. Enemy armor wasn't something that interested him.

"You will move out onto the platform and kneel," said the terrorist leader.

Pruit hesitated. He knew what was coming now. A bullet in the back of the head. Nothing he could say, nothing he could do would talk the men out of the course that they believed they had to follow. They wouldn't see it as taking a human life. It was another step in their revolution.

In the seconds that Pruit stepped out of the aircraft, he saw everything clearly. From the Jews who went quietly when the Nazis knocked on their doors, to the men who surrendered rather than fighting, knowing that the enemy didn't take prisoners. He saw mugging victims giving into the robbers rather than fighting, making the next robbery that much easier for the criminals. He knew that if everyone resisted, making robbery a risky, deadly business for the criminals, they'd find another way to get their money. He saw governments caving in to ridiculous demands, inspiring others to try a similar road.

The solution, long term, was to resist. Make it a deadly game for the terrorists and the hijackers. Playing fair with them gained nothing except copycats. Potential terrorists would see those with the courage to act on the television, their demands and message available to the whole world. They too would then plan some terrorist act.

Pruit knew that he was going to die. They were going to shoot him in the back of the head just as sure as the plane was sitting in the desert. They were going to dump his body on the tarmac so that the news minicams could photograph him lying there, the juices baking from him as his blood seeped onto the concrete, staining it crimson.

His training in the Navy had told him exactly what to do. Instructors had screamed at him, "What do you do if surrounded by five hundred enemy soldiers?"

The answer was simple. "Kill them."

It was an attitude that the best fighting forces in the world had. They knew they couldn't be defeated. Sometimes they were overwhelmed and killed, but sometimes they pulled off stunning victories. Heroic defenses that should never have worked. It was why the Japanese Navy had been turned back at Midway. Not because the Americans held an advantage but because they didn't know the meaning of defeat.

It was all attitude.

He felt the prod of a pistol in the small of his back. That was the mistake the amateur made. As it happened, Pruit whirled to the right, his elbow coming back, striking the man in the face. He twisted, grabbed at the hand holding the pistol and stepped in close. His left knee came up sharply and connected. There was a strangled cry that sounded like tires on dry concrete.

As the first man went down, his hands between his legs, a soldier leaped forward. He began raising his AK-47, but Pruit grabbed the barrel, forcing it higher as the man pulled the trigger. The barrel heated as the bullets ripped into the air. Pruit stepped in, struck with the heel of his hand. The bones on the bridge of the nose shattered. The man stumbled to the rear and fell.

Pruit spun, the AK in his hands. He fired into the door, trying to kill the terrorist leader. Below him, on the tarmac, he was aware of shouting, orders being given. He was aware of screaming inside the airplane as he opened up.

Shooting erupted all around him. Bullets snapped through the air. They struck the rail of the rolling ramp and whined off. They punched through the thin skin of the fuselage.

Pruit dropped to one knee, still firing. Inside the plane, the terrorists were diving for cover. One man was hit in the leg, the bullet tearing into his shin. Blood spurted as the man fell. He screamed and tried to roll away. Bone gleamed white through the flesh.

For a moment, Pruit thought that he was going to get away with it. He thought that the enemy, the terrorists and the soldiers would all miss him. He could win the firefight. He whirled and fired at the soldiers below him. Then a round struck him in the shoulder, spinning him. Pain blasted through his arm, shoulder and chest. He lost his grip on the AK, dropping it over the railing.

More firing erupted. The sound ran together. Bullets tore at him and the sides of the ramp. He was aware of them, but could no longer see. There was a jarring pain in his back and he thought that he fell.

The firing tapered and there was more screaming, some of it from the airplane. There were footsteps on the stairs as men ran up them. He looked up, into the barrels of two rifles and a pistol. Men were bent over him, staring down at him, their fingers tense on the triggers.

Pruit couldn't help grinning at the terrorists who had surrounded him. "I get anyone?"

There was moaning from the plane. There were two bodies in it and another four on the tarmac below. Pruit wasn't aware of them.

"No," said one of the terrorists. "You didn't get anyone except a fellow passenger. Shot him through the head killing him but you didn't hurt any of us."

Knowing that it was a lie, he tried to laugh. A final act of bravado to confuse and irritate the terrorists. It turned into a coughing spasm. He spit up blood as pain burst in his chest, almost blackening his world.

"Well, tough shit," said Pruit. "I was trying to get all you bastards."

"You're about to die and you're going to burn," said the terrorist.

"So will you," said Pruit. He coughed again and the bright lights around him faded completely. He heard voices rattling in rapid Arabic and then he heard nothing.

3

The phone was ringing when Tynan got back up to the room. He left the door standing open and rushed across the carpeting, snagging the instrument. "Yeah."

"Lieutenant Tynan?"

"Yes."

"It's me, sir. Jones."

"Did you try to call before?"

"Yes sir. That was me. I wanted to talk to you before someone higher up made the decisions that would exclude me from doing anything."

"Jones, what in the hell are you talking about?"

King entered the room and closed the door. She moved to the TV and turned it on.

"Haven't you been watching the news? Arabs hijacked another airplane."

"What does this have to do with anything?" Tynan sat down on the edge of the bed and wished that the maid hadn't turned the air conditioner on. Cold air, like an Arctic front, was blowing across the room threatening to freeze everything solid.

"I know one of the guys. Knew him before I went into the school."

That stopped Tynan for a moment and then the lieutenant asked, "How do you know he's on that plane?"

"His parents called me to ask me if I knew anything

about it. Wanted me to tell them everything I knew."

"I still don't see what this has to do with anything." He turned toward the TV where there was a Special Bulletin being broadcast, that dissolved into a picture showing a newscaster and the word *hijack*.

"Hold it," said Tynan. "Something is coming across the TV now." He snapped his fingers at King and she turned up the sound for him.

". . . ports of one man killed by the terrorists during a shootout on board the hijacked airliner. Information is sketchy but witnesses on the scene say there is one body lying on the tarmac under the plane."

Into the phone, Tynan asked, "Did you get that? They've shot one of the passengers."

"No sir. I don't have the TV on here right now. Listen, I figure that they're going to be calling in experts on this and I want to be one of those experts."

"I'm afraid," said Tynan, "I'm not going to be consulted on this one."

"Fine," said Jones. "Why can't we initiate the contact? We know what to do to end the situation. A raid at three or four in the morning, flash grenades into the aircraft. It would be easy to do."

Tynan took a deep breath. "I'm afraid that the policy on this isn't going to be left to me. People at the State Department, the Pentagon, hell, probably even the White House are going to be making the decisions. Their attitude is to negotiate with the terrorists. Don't give them anything, but talk to them until they're bored to death."

"Yes sir," said Jones. "But can't you make a few phone calls anyway?"

Tynan turned so that he wouldn't have to look at the TV screen. How many times could they show the airplane standing at the far end of the runway, surrounded by police and military vehicles, the red lights on them flashing in the setting of the desert sun? How many times could he look at it without feeling a helpless rage as men who seemed to understand nothing of the terrorist psyche tried to talk the irrational men into making rational decisions?

"There's not much I can do," said Tynan.

"Sir, there is one of ours on the plane."

"Now just what in the hell does that mean? One of our whats on the plane?"

"A SEAL, sir."

"How do you know?" asked Tynan, suddenly sick to his stomach. SEALs should not be involved on a hijacked airliner. They should be fighting in the jungles of Southeast Asia or in Africa, or somewhere else in an attempt to stop communist aggression where it appeared under the guise of freedom fighting.

"I told you, sir. I have a friend on the plane."

Tynan looked at the screen again, but now it showed a reporter interviewing a man who claimed expertise in Middle Eastern affairs.

"How do you know that your friend is on that specific plane?"

"His parents told me," Jones repeated. "Had his itinerary of his trip just in case they needed to contact him. His sister is real sick and they're not sure if she's going to survive much longer."

Tynan shook his head, thinking rapidly. There were a couple of people he could call, a couple of questions he could ask, but not much that he could do from his hotel room in Las Vegas. It was too far removed from the rest of the free world. Las Vegas was a planet all its own with different rules, a different language, and different laws.

"All right," said Tynan. "I'll see what I can do, but I can't promise you anything. Where are you going to be?"

Jones gave him a number and said, "If I'm not here, you can leave a message for me."

"Okay. I'll see what I can learn." When Jones thanked him, he hung up and looked at King. "That was Jones."

"So I gathered. What's the deal?"

Tynan kicked off his shoes and rocked back, against the pillows at the head of the bed. He stared at the TV which had slipped back to a game show where a heavy woman was jumping around like a teenager on hot concrete.

"Jones thinks he knows one of the passengers on the plane and wants me to make a call to see if we can arrange some kind of rescue for the passengers."

"You going to do it?"

Tynan rubbed a hand over his face and then shrugged. "I don't think there is much that I can do. By the time we could get the team together, learn what was happening, the whole episode would probably be over."

King sat down on the corner of the bed closest to him. She turned so that she could look at Tynan. "Then you're going to do nothing."

"You have an idea, you could let me in on it."

She glanced at the TV and then at him. "Seems to me that you could at least find out what is going on."

"Stevie, they're not going to tell me anything on the phone. Not a secure line. We want to learn anything, we're going to have to leave Vegas. You want to do that?"

"We can come back."

Tynan sighed and then sat up. "Look, the logistics of the situation are such that there really is nothing that I can do before the hijacking will end. At most, these things last ten, twelve hours."

"And no one gets hurt?" she said.

"Well that has been the pattern until now."

Again the game show was interrupted. The Special Bulletin sign came on and then the newscaster was back.

"We've just learned the identity of the man killed by the terrorists on the hijacked aircraft. A spokesman on the aircraft, identifying himself only as a representative of the October the Twenty-seventh Faction, has claimed that Seaman Allen Pruit was killed as an enemy of freedom loving peoples everywhere. A spokesman for the Pentagon has confirmed that Pruit was on the flight. He is identified as an Underwater Demolitions Expert assigned in Italy."

"Oh, Christ," said Tynan.

"What?"

"UDT. That's how they identify us to the civilian world that doesn't know about the SEALs. Jones was right. He is one of our boys."

Just as he said that, the phone began to ring again.

With the suitcases locked and stacked near the door, and with King searching the drawers to make sure that she had forgotten nothing, Tynan asked, "Are you sure that you don't mind if we cut this short?"

"No, Mark. It's fine. Besides, I'm getting a trip to Washington DC out of it. I'll trade the heat of the desert here for the heat of Washington."

"We got everything?"

"I don't see anything lying around," she said. "I've got everything that I came with."

There was a knock at the door and the bellboy was there. He loaded the luggage onto a cart and pushed it away. King left the room and Tynan closed the door as he stepped into the hallway to follow them.

"I didn't get a chance to play roulette while we were here," she said.

"Neither did I."

They took the elevator down to the lobby and Tynan checked out quickly. They moved through the doors and took a cab that was waiting outside the door out to the airport. In no time, he'd got them tickets on an east bound flight with a layover in Dallas of three hours. He wasn't happy with that, but it was the fastest available flight to Washington DC. The only way he could have gotten there faster was to drive to Nellis Air Force Base and catch a military hop. That would leave King in Vegas to find her own way out to Washington. He didn't see how a couple of hours would make that much difference.

They got on the plane, waited on the ground for a few minutes and then took off. Tynan leaned back, his eyes on the window, looking out into the cloudless, blue sky as they climbed higher. The captain came on telling them that they would be flying over the Grand Canyon so that everyone would have a chance to look at it from the air.

Tynan wasn't interested in that. He'd seen it on the way in. Now he was more concerned with the other airplane, sitting on a runway in Libya. Before they had boarded, he'd learned that it was still there and that nothing had changed radically. The terrorists had made more demands. Prisoners from Israel, safe conduct to another airport and a promise that no one would follow them. For that, they'd release the children, some of the women, but they'd hold everyone else until they arrived at their new destination. Unlike other hijackings, it didn't seem that this one was going to be over quickly.

King leaned over and asked quietly, "How are you going to go about this?"

"That's a good question," said Tynan. "The major problem is that Libya is a hostile environment for us. We can't count on help from the local government so we have to engineer a way to get onto the field without alerting the enemy. We also need a plan of the plane, where the emergency exits are, what doors can be opened and which cannot. And it would be helpful to know where all the passengers are."

"I hadn't thought of that," she said.

"There are probably a hundred things that you haven't thought of. If, for some reason, the hijackers have buckets of jet fuel sitting in the aisles, we can't use flash grenades. Shooting could set it off. We have to worry about the fuel tanks and if they're ruptured. We don't know how many terrorists are on board or what they look like."

"The terrorists will be the ones holding the guns," she told him.

Tynan smiled and said, "That's not always true. I know of one hostage situation where the hostage was given an unloaded pistol so that it would look as if he was leading out another hostage. The real terrorist had his hands up as they emerged from the building."

"Oh."

Tynan looked at her and then across the aisle where a young woman sat, her eyes wide in fright. "Hey, we're talking about a movie plot here, nothing more."

"Sure," said the woman, swallowing audibly. "Sure."

Tynan sat back in his seat and stared out the window. King put her hand on his arm but didn't ask him any more questions. The stewardesses came around, provided them with a Coke and then left to prepare the lunch. They served it and then cleaned up that mess. By the time they finished, they had arrived in Dallas for the three hour layover. Tynan got off to find a newspaper and then returned to the plane.

"Any news?" asked King.

"None. Plane's still on the ground. Demands are the same, though they have sent in some food."

The second hop to Washington seemed to take almost no time. Tynan studied everything in the newspaper, trying to learn some more about the situation. He knew that there would be a great deal more information available through the various intelligence agencies. They would have sources inside the Libyan government, and there might be information available through the Mossad, the Israeli intelligence organization. None of that would be available to the press.

They landed in the dark at Washington's National Airport. Tynan was surprised that it was night until he remembered that Las Vegas was three hours behind Washington DC.

They got off the plane and made their way toward the

baggage claim area. As they walked along the concourse, jammed with hundreds of others, Tynan heard his name called once. He turned and saw Jones moving through the crowd toward him.

"I've got a car arranged and we're due at the State Department in about an hour."

Tynan looked at the younger man. He was in his early twenties, tall, thin with light hair. His skin was deeply tanned from his time at sea and on land in various tropical environments. A talented young man, with an ability to build a working radio from tin cans and wires. Smarter than most people but who had been bored with the mundane life in the workaday Navy. He had joined the SEALs for the training and the adventure they offered.

Tynan stuck out his hand and said, "Good evening, Jones. Moving a bit fast aren't you?"

"No sir. Reported in and learned that someone had suggested putting together a team. I indicated that we had one coming in now and we inherited the job."

Tynan looked at all the people circulating around them. "I don't like this," he said.

"Nothing not to like, sir. We'll get your bags, drop Stevie off at the hotel on the way into town and be to the State Department in plenty of time."

"How'd you learn that something was being planned?"

"Nothing to it," said Jones as he turned and began walking toward the terminal. "They, meaning the State Department, queried the Navy as to who might be available and the chief in charge there called me. Simple."

They came to the baggage claim area and waited. Tynan said, "I don't like the way this is coming together. Much too haphazard. No one has thought the thing through."

"It's all been laid out. The problem is speed," said Jones. "We've got to be on the plane later tonight."

"No," said Tynan. "Not until we have a better idea of what is happening there. The last thing we need to do is ride in with guns blazing. That just doesn't work."

Jones lowered his voice as he looked around to make sure that no one was listening. "Hijackers released a couple of the passengers and we've learned some things from them. You'll see in a few minutes."

They recovered their luggage and Jones lead them out, into the hot, muggy night. Insects were thick, swarming around the lights on the poles in the parking lot. Some of them swooped down, dive bombing Tynan and King. She swung her hand around her face, trying to chase them away.

Jones found his car, a gray, stripped four door model from the interagency pool. They tossed the luggage into the trunk and then climbed in, King in the backseat, Tynan in the front and Jones behind the wheel. He started it and then rolled down the window.

"No air conditioning."

"Perfect," said Tynan.

Twenty minutes later, they dropped King off at the hotel with orders to secure the rooms. Jones then pulled out into traffic again and drove to the State Department.

"Don't want to alert the press," he explained, "by having the meeting at the Pentagon. Easier to disguise the nature of it here."

"Perfect," said Tynan.

They parked and walked into the building. The guard there stopped them, found their names on the access list and told them that everyone else had arrived. They walked across the brightly lighted, tiled lobby and stopped in front of the elevator doors. When the elevator arrived, they took it up to the seventh floor. Once there, they walked down the hallway, past the closed and locked doors of offices vacated for the evening. The lights had been cut down so that it was dim in the corridor. Pools of light and areas of gloom.

At the end of the hall was an oasis of light and a wall of

noise. People talking to one another, shouting, and looking as if they planned to head on home as quickly as possible once the meeting ended.

Jones and Tynan entered the conference room where there were twenty or thirty people. The conference table in the center of the room was littered with coffee cups, the remains of sandwiches and ashtrays that were overflowing. There were file folders and papers scattered everywhere. Copies of *The New York Times* and *The Washington Post* were spread around. In one corner were two television sets, one sitting on top of the other, each turned to a different station for the latest news. No one was paying any attention to them.

Jones walked in and looked into the faces of the men and women gathered around. He pointed out a couple to Tynan and then dragged the lieutenant toward the head of the table.

"Mr. Scarlotti, this is Lieutenant Tynan, the man I told you about."

"Yes, Lieutenant. Good of you to come. I'm afraid that it is a wasted trip. We've decided that there is no way that you or your men could be deployed. Your end of the operation has been scrubbed and you're free to return to your regular duties."

"Perfect," said Tynan.

4

Standing in the lobby of the brightly lighted building, staring out into the muggy heat of the Washington evening, Jones asked, "You going to leave it at that?"

"What the hell do you expect me to do?"

Jones rubbed his face. He glanced at the desk, thirty feet away where the guard sat watching a small black and white television. "Sir, that was a Navy SEAL those assholes gunned down. We can't let them get away with that."

Tynan scratched his head. He watched the traffic flowing past the building. A limousine cruised by, slowed and turned a corner. There were no flags on the fenders so it probably wasn't anyone very important.

"There's not much that we can do," he said finally.

"Sure there is. You can talk to some people in the Pentagon. We can attack the problem from another angle."

Tynan looked at his watch and said, "Not tonight we can't. It's too late and no one is going to appreciate a wake up call on this."

"Afraid you'll ruin their beauty sleep," snapped Jones sarcastically.

"Politically speaking," said Tynan, "you do not get favors by irritating the people in the position to grant them. You barge in, screaming and hollering, and the people are going to ignore you and resist your ideas. You show up, hat in hand and show them how they can look good, and

31

you just might find the authorization for your plan."

"But we're running out of time."

"Jones, there is nothing that could be accomplished this late anyway. You said that we've a team in place. I've seen no evidence of that."

"Well, I took the liberty of calling in a few friends who'd want to go along. Talked to Jacobs and a guy you don't know named Strong. And then there's a couple of other guys here in Washington that we could get, if we need some extra help to pull this off."

"I don't know," said Tynan.

"Come on, sir. Those bastards killed a SEAL. Gunned him down. We're supposed to be this elite fighting force, full of esprit, so tough that fifteen of the enemy aren't enough to take one of us."

"In a fair fight," Tynan reminded him. "Not when we're on an airliner, unarmed."

"Makes no difference, sir. We've got to do something about it."

For a long time Tynan said nothing. He just watched the traffic outside. Across the street a couple walked along looking into the windows of the office buildings almost as if they were window shopping. There were some interesting displays in the windows. Recruiting posters for the military or the civil service, a diorama that showed how nuclear power would improve the environment, and a placard advertising an upcoming concert on the mall.

Tynan was thinking about what Jones had said. He was right. The SEALs were an elite fighting force, tougher, smarter, quicker than any other fighting force on Earth. They took care of their own. If one SEAL needed help, then all the others would come running as quickly as they could.

Now, the man in Libya couldn't be helped. He was dead. But the code demanded that they get even. They had to go to Libya to end the hijacking. That was the only thing they could do because it would undermine the morale of the SEALs to do anything less.

"I want you to call those men you know and have them meet somewhere tomorrow morning for breakfast. Doesn't matter where, but stay there until I get back to you. If we have to move, we're going to have to do it quickly."

"Aye aye, sir."

"But there is really nothing to do until tomorrow morning. Can you pick me up tomorrow morning for a trip over to the Pentagon?"

"No problem."

"Then let's get the hell out of here."

Susan Calhern sat sweating in the rear of the stinking jet aircraft and thought that it should have cooled off during the night. She had always been told that the night in the desert was cold, but there was nothing here that suggested the theory was right. It was as hot in the plane as it had been from almost the moment the pilot had turned off the engines and the air conditioning.

She was in a seat made for three, but sitting with five. Crammed in there so that the terrorists would be able to keep an eye on them easily. They had received no food since the plane landed, had been given a cup of water and allowed into the restroom that had quickly become an overflowing, reeking area because of the situation.

There had been gunfire up front. There had been cries of pain and rumors that one of the passengers had been killed. When the shooting stopped, the terrorists had burst through the curtain and threatened to shoot everyone. They had dragged a couple of young women to the front and shouted that they would be shot in retribution.

That hadn't happened yet, though the women had been beaten. Several of the men were beaten too, their cries rippling through the plane and seeming to echo along the fuselage, making everyone tense.

Calhern, like the others, had sat there quietly, trying to be invisible. But she was a tall woman with long, red-blond hair, an angular face with fine features, and skin that burned so easily she tried to stay out of the sun. She had noticed one of the terrorists kept eyeing her. Afraid to make eye contact, she stared out the window until the terrorists made them close all the shades. Then she watched the floor or the back of the seat in front of her.

And sweated. Like everyone else. The temperature in the plane climbed steadily, until some of the older passengers were moaning. A few had passed out, but the terrorists had done nothing for them. One woman stripped off her blouse, sitting in only her bra, the sweat dripping down her body. It hadn't seemed to cool her at all, but it did attract the attention of the terrorists. Calhern wanted to avoid that.

"When are you going to let us go?" wailed a woman.

One of the terrorists moved toward her and stood staring down at her. He fingered the trigger of his weapon and said, calmly, almost quietly, "It is not us. It is the officials. They refuse to negotiate in good faith with us. You must blame them for the failure."

The woman nodded and didn't speak again. Her face had gone completely white.

As the man turned, another of the terrorists entered the cabin carrying a number of passports. He held them aloft and said, "I have here the documents of all the Americans, the French, the British, the Canadians, and the Jews. We are going to hold a drawing and the winner gets to perform for the television cameras."

He turned and faced one of the older women. "Here. You make the choice."

"No," she said quietly, refusing to look up. "I couldn't do that."

"You can do it," said the terrorist kindly. "Either draw one of the passports, or you shall be selected."

"Please," she said. She glanced up, her face stained with tears.

"You draw. Now."

Tentatively, she reached out. She touched one passport and then another.

"Hey!" shouted a woman. "She can tell nationality by the colors."

"Shut up!" ordered one of the terrorists.

The leader, however, said, "That's right. You turn your head and make a selection."

A silence descended on the plane then. The people were trying to see what was happening with the woman who had to make the selections, but no one was saying a word. It was as if they believed that talking would somehow cause her to grab the passport with that person's name on it. Silence was the key to remaining anonymous.

The woman hesitated, reaching and then dropping her hand. Her shoulders shook as she cried quietly, helplessly.

"Are you volunteering for the activity?" asked the terrorist leader.

Without a word, she grabbed one of the passports and held it up for him. He took it, opened it and said, "We have a winner. Oh, and what a pretty winner too."

Some of the women, slumped back in their seats, relieved. Normally, they would have been insulted to not be thought of as pretty, but now it had become a survival trait. They were too old, overweight, skinny, or wrinkled to be considered pretty and they were happy for it.

The terrorist leader marched down the aisle, waving the passport in front of him. He glanced right and left, staring into the eyes of those women he held captive. He stopped once, looked at a woman with long, black hair and then shook his head. The relief was unmistakable in that woman's face.

When he reached the rear of the aircraft, he stopped and waited. He watched as the women squirmed and sweated and prayed that he didn't hold the passport with their name.

"Susan Calhern," he said finally.

Calhern, for an instant, thought he'd said something else. Thought that he'd called someone else. And then the blood drained from her face and the cabin spun. She thought she was going to pass out, and then thought that she was going to be sick.

"Come on, Calhern. You don't want us to get nasty do you?"

She stood slowly, waited as the others crammed into the seat with her shifted around and then moved to the aisle. As she reached it, she turned and faced that man at the rear of the aircraft.

"This is you, isn't it?" he asked. He held her passport so that she could see the picture of herself staring back from the small document.

"Yes," she said so softly that it was nearly inaudible. She swallowed and said again, "Yes."

He moved forward and pushed her on the shoulder, turning her. They marched up the aisle quickly. No one spoke as they passed through the curtain into the first class cabin. There, a couple of the men looked up at her. Most of them had bruises on their faces and blood splattered on their shirts. A woman lay on the floor in a fetal position, whimpering.

Then she looked forward. The feet of one of the terrorists killed in the firefight was sticking out of the galley at the front of the plane. Blood was splashed on the bulkheads and on the floor. Calhern felt her stomach turn over and thought that she was going to throw up.

Through the open door, on the ramp pushed up against the side of the jet, she saw bullet holes. The doorway was riddled and covered in blood.

"The other American has made it tougher on the rest of you," he said.

"But . . ."

"Face the door," commanded the terrorist.

When she did, he grabbed her hands and pulled them behind her back, lashing them together with a thin leather cord. The binding wasn't tight and given a few moments, she was sure that she could free herself. She didn't try it with the terrorists watching her.

She was then pushed out onto the ramp. She stood there, in the open air and stared down at the vague shapes of the military vehicles, hidden by the darkness. The odor of blood was thick around her.

"Kneel," commanded the terrorist.

She did as told, being careful not to lose her balance and trying to avoid the blood. As she knelt, the bright lights from a TV camera crew came on. She blinked and turned her face away from the lights.

"Now you will learn the power we hold."

She felt a pistol pushed up against the back of her head. She heard the hammer drawn back and she knew that she was going to die.

As soon as Tynan opened the door, King asked him, "How'd it go?"

"Not good. State Department, or whoever it was, decided that they didn't want to offend the terrorists. We're not going to do a thing."

King picked up a glass from the combination dresser and desk and handed it to Tynan. "Took the liberty of making this for you."

"Thanks. Anything on the TV?"

She glanced at it and said, "Nothing new. Terrorists are making demands and the governments are trying to negotiate. Everything is on hold, although the terrorists have issued a deadline for the next concession."

Tynan gulped at his drink and then sat down on the corner of the bed. "You can't negotiate with these guys."

"What would you do?" asked King.

"You mean how would I end this ordeal or stop the hijackers from doing it again?"

"What's the difference?" asked King.

"The difference is, if I have a short term goal, it is to get those passengers out alive. Long term, those passengers don't mean a thing. I want to keep this from happening again."

King picked up her own drink and took a deep swallow. "You mean you'd kill the passengers."

Tynan grinned, but it was an evil look. "The moment I heard a plane was hijacked, I'd shoot it down. And when the next one was hijacked, I'd shoot it down. I'd keep the media from reporting the hijackers' demands, though I would be sure to let them know that we planned to shoot down the airplanes."

"And kill a hundred, two hundred innocent people."

"Now, but we'd save hundreds later."

"Jesus, Mark, you can't be serious."

He took another long pull at his drink and said, "If the terrorists learned that we weren't even going to talk to them, that a hijacking resulted in their deaths immediately and that their cause would get no play in the media, then the phenomena would end abruptly."

"But to just shoot down . . ."

"Not very realistic, is it? Second plan. Don't negotiate with them under any circumstances. Storm the plane and free as many of the hostages as possible but make sure all the terrorists die in the attack . . ."

"Without a trial?"

"You're talking about civilization and I'm talking about terrorists. You cannot deal with them. You have to kill them. When they understand that their terrorist acts are going to result in their deaths, they'll stop it."

She moved toward the window and looked out. Then she turned and said, "You're not serious."

"Oh, somewhat," said Tynan. "The solution is to not let them hold people hostage and to make sure retribution is swift and deadly. Now, we let them have all the cards and the more ruthless they are, the more space they get."

"So what are you going to do?" she asked.

"About this situation in Libya? I don't know what I'm going to do. Tomorrow, I'll talk to a few people and see if we can get authorization to move on the plane. I think we can take it without getting any of the passengers killed. It'll take coordination to do it, but it can be done."

"And the terrorists?" she asked.

Tynan looked at her and knew what she wanted to hear. She was a college professor who had a somewhat rose colored view of the world. She saw things as they should be. But that was if everyone acted as they should. Too many people operated only in their own self-interest and if someone got in the way, they were crushed.

"We take them prisoner," said Tynan. "If that is possible without endangering either my men or the passengers."

"Then what was all that stuff about shooting down the plane?"

Tynan finished his drink. "I want you to think about this. See the terrorists for what they are. Cowards like the school yard bully who picks on the smaller kids. Terrorists are not idealists or purists. They are thugs bent on grabbing glory for themselves in the name of some cause. Now, if they know, believe, that we're not even going to talk, but we'll shoot, they'll have to stop their acts of violence. It gains them nothing in the end but death."

"There are some who don't mind dying for their cause," she said.

"True fanatics," agreed Tynan, "but there aren't many of them. Most of them have an escape plan and if the odds are upped to include their deaths, the situations would be reversed."

"But what about the innocent people?" she asked again.

"There's the fly in the ointment. We worry about the innocent people. The terrorists don't. That's the power they hold over us. Our desire is to get the innocents out of the situation before they are injured."

"So what are you going to do?" she asked.

"Tomorrow I'm going in to talk and see if I can convince anyone in the Pentagon that we need to make a move to end the situation, providing it doesn't resolve itself tonight."

King moved to where she could look at the television screen. "If you make no hostile move, then the hostages will be freed, eventually."

"Not the point," said Tynan. But he knew that she'd never see his point and he doubted that she'd convince him that negotiation was the path to follow. Not when every move and countermove was reported internationally because that gave the terrorists the one thing they craved. Worldwide attention.

"Hey," she said and pointed at the screen.

The camera was focused, from a long way, on the door at the front of the jet. The stairway was in place and kneeling on the top of it was a woman, her hands tied behind her. The terrorist, a thin man in khaki held a pistol at her head. For a few moments nothing happened.

5

The taxi, rather than Jones, let Tynan out at the front steps that lead up into the largest office building in the world. A solid, gray stone structure that had little in the way of decoration on the front of it. Rows and rows of windows, stretching in both directions that gave the impression of going on forever. A massive structure that rivaled the great pyramid at Teotihuacán in the Valley of Mexico or the giant one on the banks of the Nile. He stood at the foot of the steps, like an archaeologist about to enter into the tomb of an ancient king. He felt as well equipped to enter the Pentagon as some of those archaeologists were to enter the tombs.

He walked up the steps, opened one of the massive doors and entered. He flashed his military ID card at a guard and entered one of the many tiled corridors that filled the building. Miles of them, laid out in a complex, confusing fashion as if the architect's plan had been to fool enemy spies, should one somehow penetrate the outer ring.

And there was an odor in the building that was unlike that of anywhere else in the world. It wasn't quite like that of a locker room. More like a combination of sweat and paper and dust and copier fluid. A strange, sickly sweet odor that wasn't overpowering. It crept up on you, from a distance until suddenly you were aware of it. Tynan noticed it as he walked in the door, but only because he had been inside the Pentagon a dozen times before.

He worked his way through the labyrinth of corridors and cross corridors until he found himself outside the office of Commander William P. Good, a man Tynan had known for two or three years. Given Good's job, as one of the many liaison officers dealing with the Secretary of Defense, it seemed to be the perfect place to start.

He opened the door, found a civilian secretary sitting at a battleship gray desk that might have been used during the Civil War. A young woman with short cropped hair and huge glasses and who was drinking coffee.

"Yes?" she asked.

"I'd like to see the commander."

"You have an appointment?"

Tynan shook his head. "Just tell him that Lieutenant Tynan would like a few minutes of his time."

"Of course." She stood and opened the door that was to her right. Hers was a small office with barely enough room for her desk, a small bookcase and two chairs for visitors. Obviously Good wasn't a very important cog in the great Pentagon machine. But then he did rate a secretary.

She returned, smiled politely, and said, "The commander will see you now."

Tynan stepped to the door and opened it. The inner office wasn't much bigger than the outer, but the desk was dark wood instead of metal, and there was carpeting on the floor. File cabinets stood off to one side, there were visitor's chairs in front of the desk and a couple paintings of sailing ships on the walls.

Before Tynan could get through the door, Good was on his feet and moving around the desk. "Mark! What in the hell are you doing here?"

Tynan reached out to shake hands with his friend. That was the thing about the Navy. No matter where you went, you could always find someone you knew. Maybe you'd only spent a week together at a school, or served for a couple of months at sea, but there was always someone.

"I'm in town for a couple of days."

Good gestured at one of the chairs. "Sit. Sit. Can I get you some coffee?"

"Coffee would be good," said Tynan.

Good moved to the door, leaned out and said something to his secretary. He returned, sat in the other chair. "So, how have you been?"

"Great," said Tynan. "You?"

"Got married about two years ago. Beautiful lady named Debbie. Keeps me on the straight and narrow."

"Say, congratulations."

"Thank you. You married?"

"No. Still moving around too often. Navy keeps me hopping on special assignments."

"I heard something about that. Just what do you do?" asked Good.

"That's a question I haven't given a straight answer to in a long time. Have to make up things . . ."

"Don't tell me you're one of those SEALs."

Now Tynan grinned. "Then you've heard."

"You boys are supposed to be very tough. Doesn't seem to fit you."

The door opened and the secretary entered carrying a tray. She paused in front of Tynan, let him grab a cup, dump in some sugar, and then gave him a chance to get a pastry if he wanted. Tynan shook his head no. She then served her boss and retreated without ever saying a word.

Tynan tasted the coffee and said, "Not bad."

"One of the advantages of working here," said Good. "Good coffee and no one shoots at you."

"Speaking of which," began Tynan.

"Oh-oh," said Good. "Maybe I should move back to my desk."

"Not that serious," said Tynan. "I just need some guidance from you."

Good sipped his coffee, studying Tynan over the top of his cup, and said, "What do you need to know?"

"Well," said Tynan, "you're familiar with the situation that is developing in Libya."

"If you mean the hijacking, then yes. But only what I've read in the newspapers. Nothing else."

Tynan took another drink and said, "I'd like to propose that we put a team in the field to resolve the terrorist situation in Libya."

"Shit, Mark, get serious."

"I am serious."

Good stood up and moved to his desk, sitting in the chair behind it. It was almost as if he was telling Tynan that the visit was over and that Good was going back to work.

"All I need is a point in the right direction," said Tynan. "Someone who could look at a plan and have the authority to approve the mission."

"I don't see," said Good, "how you could get anything into the field in time to be of any benefit. Hell, Mark, these things don't last all that long."

"Bill, this one's been going on for over twenty-four hours and they've released none of the passengers. I think we've entered a new phase in terrorism. They've killed a passenger and threatened another."

"What do you hope to accomplish?" asked Good. "Your training isn't in this sort of thing."

Tynan grinned. He knew that his friend had at least a secret security clearance. All officers had that much. But given his rank and his position in the Pentagon, Good probably was cleared for Top Secret. But then, Tynan wasn't authorized to spread secrets about the SEALs, even if Good was already familiar with the unit.

"We've had a few classes on how to seize military objectives with a minimum loss of life on both sides," said

Tynan. That was certainly non-committal enough. "That could be adapted to this situation easily."

"Damn, Mark." Good looked up at the door, making sure that it was locked. "Damn." He hesitated for a moment. "I misled you. I have seen a couple of classified reports. Not much more in them than you'd see in the paper, except to suggest that the Libyan government might be supporting the hijackers. Now, how does that affect your mission?"

Tynan shrugged. "Look, Bill, all I want to do is look at this, see if there is something that I can do and then present it to the right place."

Good rocked back in his chair and sipped at his coffee. He set the cup down and said, "All right. I'll take you upstairs to Commander Keogh's office. You can talk to him and see if there is anything for you to do."

"Thanks, Bill, I appreciate it."

Calhern sat leaning forward so that her weight wasn't resting on her bound hands. She was surprised that she was still alive. She was surprised that no one had protested her being escorted out for execution.

She'd knelt there, in the blood of the man who had died earlier, sweat soaking her light dress. She was intensely aware of everything around her. Of the heat, the darkness, the quiet buzzing of insects, of the men and vehicles just off the tarmac and inside the fence.

When the barrel had been pushed against her neck, she was sure the end was near. But the time passed. The pressure from the weapon didn't slacken. Her knees began to hurt from the hard metal of the ramp. Her shoulders ached but she was afraid to move. Afraid that the slightest motion would make the terrorist shoot her.

The lights of the camera, somewhere beyond the ring of military vehicles, went out, leaving her in the dark. As that happened, the pressure from the pistol relaxed. It was still against her head, but the man was no longer pushing on it.

For an eternity, she knelt there, staring at the black stain against the lighter metal and wondered if she would even know if the trigger was pulled. Would she feel anything, or would the world suddenly go black? The funny thing was that she wasn't scared. Her mind was dealing with the situation on an intellectual level.

One of the terrorists pulled her to her feet. He managed to grab her breasts, squeezing them painfully, but she refused to react to his touch. The man pushed her back into the plane where she stood waiting for instructions from the terrorists.

Suddenly she felt weak. Her knees were shaking and she felt tears spring to her eyes. She fell against the bulkhead and took a single, deep breath.

"We have decided that the time is not right," said the terrorist leader. "We have decided to show our compassion and have granted a reprieve. It is now up to the governments to see that you continue to live."

No one bothered to untie her hands. They pushed her into the front seat in the first class section. There was no one else in those chairs. They had been forced into the seats directly behind her.

"Please," she said as she sat down. She leaned so that the terrorists could see her bound hands, but none of them moved to free her. When they didn't, she sat back defiantly.

Now, the sun was up again and the fuselage was baking again. The metal was popping as the sun struck it, heating it rapidly. Sunlight streamed in the open door, almost as if to spotlight the bloodstains on the deck and on the bulkhead. As it heated, the smell of the blood filled the first class cabin.

Still no one had offered to untie her. She still thought that she could get free if she worked at it, but didn't want to offend her captors. If she freed her hands, it might make them mad enough to shoot her. So she sat there, leaning forward, and waited, just as everyone else did.

Good didn't stay long after he introduced Tynan to Keogh. He bowed out quickly. Keogh was a slender man with short gray hair, a tiny moustache and a look of discomfort on his face. Tynan wondered if the man was sick. He gestured at the chair in front of his desk and Tynan dropped into it.

The office was almost a carbon copy of the one occupied by Good. A single desk, a couple of chairs for visitors, a short bookcase and paintings of sailing ships on the walls.

"Now, Lieutenant," said Keogh as he moved the papers and files around his desk. "What can I do for you?"

Tynan wasn't prepared for this. He'd known what he needed to say but he wasn't prepared to say it. The major problem was that most of the information he had to give to establish his credibility would be classified and he didn't know if Keogh was cleared to hear it. Then again, if there was more information available about the hijacking, it too would be classified and the problem would reverse itself.

"Lieutenant," prompted Keogh.

"Yes sir. You are aware of the hijacking in Libya?"

"Of course." He grinned, showing yellowed teeth. "It's in all the papers."

"Well, sir, several men and I have come up with an idea that might end the situation a little faster than negotiation seems to be working."

"So?"

Tynan shrugged. "So, if we can put our plan into operation, there is a good chance that we could get the people out alive and destroy the morale of the terrorists."

"And what do you want me to do about it?"

"I need to talk with someone with the authority to approve the plan and help us get the ball rolling." Tynan was aware that he was repeating himself. He'd told Good the same thing and Good had handed him off to Keogh. Tynan realized that Keogh wouldn't have the authority to authorize the mission. He'd just have the authority to either kill it or bounce it another rung up the ladder.

"Just what do you have in mind?"

"A few trained men to sneak aboard the plane, eliminate the terrorists and free the hostages. Swift and quiet. Move at night and take them by surprise."

"You are trained to do this?"

Tynan shrugged. "Hell, I'm trained to slip up on enemy installations and take out the guards without alerting the soldiers inside. This is the same thing, only there are fewer men to take out."

"You are aware that our government is not directly involved in the negotiations with the terrorists and that there are only a few Americans on board the plane. The majority of the passengers are Jewish, Indian and Arab."

"So?" asked Tynan.

"There is no one in the Pentagon, hell, I doubt that there is anyone in the Department of Defense, who could give you the permission you need."

Tynan leaned back in his chair and stared at the man. He crossed his legs and then asked, "You telling me that I'm not to take this request higher?"

"Lieutenant, I'm telling you that you could go to the President himself and not get permission. It isn't our problem. It's the problem of the Libyans, and the Italians and the Israelis."

"There are Americans on that plane," said Tynan.

"Not that many."

"All right," said Tynan. "Then what about the man who was murdered? He was an American."

"If I understand the story right, he grabbed a weapon

and started shooting at the terrorists. He was killed in the fight that followed."

Tynan started to smile at the news but then controlled it. Keogh wouldn't understand. Tynan was proud of the man. He didn't give up but tried to do something about the situation. It would be interesting to learn exactly how many of the enemy, of the terrorists died in the firefight. It might not have done the man any good, but it sure as hell had to mess up their plan.

"Even so," said Tynan. "Nothing would have happened if the terrorists hadn't taken over the plane. Now, we've got to do something to end the situation."

"No, Lieutenant," said Keogh, "that is exactly what we don't have to do. This situation is not for us to solve. We just have to sit back and let others take the heat."

"Even if we can end it?"

Keogh wiped a hand over his face and then pulled a handkerchief from his hip pocket. As he rubbed his hands on it, he said, "Even if we could go in and free everyone without anyone getting hurt, we won't do it. It's not our problem to solve."

"Not our problem," repeated Tynan.

Keogh leaned forward, his elbows on the desk. "Listen, there are things going on that you don't know about, aren't required to know about and aren't authorized to know about. Let's just say that your quest for permission has ended here."

"I don't have your permission to see your boss and try to talk him into letting us make a stab at it."

"No, you do not," said Keogh. "Let me make myself perfectly clear on this point. Commando raids into Libya are not authorized. We must respect the sovereignty of that nation. If they request assistance, then I'm sure that we'll render it, but until that time, there is nothing for us to do. Nothing that we can do."

"Commander," asked Tynan, "just what sort of aid would we provide?"

"Hostage negotiators. Men who have experience in dealing with terrorists and hostage situations. Men who will be able to negotiate an end to this hijacking without the terrorists gaining their objectives."

Tynan laughed. "What if all these demands they're making now is a smoke screen? What if they're only interested in the press coverage of the hijacking?"

"Then they have succeeded in accomplishing their mission," said Keogh.

"Exactly," said Tynan. "Now, what if they all died and the hostages were freed. How would that look to the world after the press reported it?"

"The mission failed."

"Exactly," repeated Tynan. "We have the chance to snatch a victory here with a bold, aggressive plan. We can do it. We have the trained people."

"No, Lieutenant, we don't. I don't mean the people aren't trained and available, I mean that we don't have the opportunity for any type of independent action. Your idea has already been discussed at higher levels and rejected. To bring it up again, after it has been examined, would only irritate the brass here and there is no reason to do that."

Tynan sat there quietly for a moment, his mind racing as he thought about it. Finally he said, "You're saying that I'm not to take this higher."

"I don't know how to make it any clearer. Your best course of action, hell, your only course of action is to get your butt out of my office before I get pissed off, and forget you ever came in here. I'll do the same and we'll both have a chance for promotion."

"But, sir . . ."

"No buts on this one. It's all over now. You've lost. Strike your colors and get out."

Tynan hesitated and then stood up. He saluted and then

spun, heading toward the door. He stopped there, with his hand on the knob and thought about telling Keogh he was going to try upstairs, but knew it was a hollow gesture. Keogh could make one phone call and Tynan wouldn't even be allowed into the offices there. The SPs would be called and he would be escorted from the building. His service jacket would be marked and he would find his military career stifled, all for a gesture of defiance that would gain him nothing. He still wouldn't get in to see the higher ranking officers, and if he did, the answer would be the same.

He opened the door and left the office, not knowing what he was going to do. The only course left was to tell Jones and the others and then head back out on leave. There was nothing else he could do.

6

Tynan took a cab into downtown Washington, in search of the restaurant where Jones and the others waited for the word. Sitting in the back, listening to the sounds of the traffic around him, Tynan tried to figure out what to say to his men. They weren't going to be happy with the decision. They weren't going to like the fact that no one would even listen to him and that the plan had been shot down before it had gotten off the ground.

The taxi glided to the right and pulled over. Tynan leaned over the front seat, handing the driver a ten dollar bill that more than paid the fare and provided a generous tip. He got out and looked at the brick and glass front of the restaurant. There was a parking lot to one side and a row of short green bushes that lined the sidewalk to the front door. A homey little place that probably catered to tourists rather than the high powered Washington clientele.

He pushed open the door and stepped into the air conditioned comfort and moved toward a podium that held menus and a sign that said, "Please wait to be seated."

In the rear, sitting in a booth stuck in the corner, Tynan saw Thomas Jones and Jake Jacobs. Jacobs was a big man, with whom Tynan had worked before. Dark hair and a deep tan gave him a Latin look, but when he spoke, his deep Southern accent eliminated the impression. He wore civilian clothes with a shirt that looked as if a paint factory had exploded as he walked past it.

Jones stood and waved and Tynan headed over toward their table waving off the hostess who was coming to escort him into the restaurant.

When he was seated, a glass of water by his hand and a menu lying in front of him, Jones pointed to the two men that Tynan didn't recognize. "This is Kenneth Strong."

Tynan reached across the table to shake hands with the man. A large man with light blond hair that was thinning on top. There was a hint of a mustache on his lip. He had blue eyes and sharp features.

"And this other man is Tim Webster."

Webster was shorter and darker than Strong. He had thick black hair and deeply tanned skin. There was a white scar on his forehead and another on his chin. He had brown eyes, a pointed nose and ears that looked like jug handles.

"Webster."

"Skipper."

Jones took a drink of his water and then said, "Well?"

"Well, nothing. Got shot down before I even had the chance to pitch the story. I was fed a line about negotiations being handled at a high level and that it wasn't the responsibility of the United States to get involved."

"And you listened to that?"

"There comes a point when it is no longer possible to push a plan without danger."

"Oh," said Jones. "Worried about your career."

Tynan took a drink of water, his eyes on the younger man. "That is not fair."

For an instant Jones sat staring back and then dropped his eyes. "Sorry, Skipper."

"What it meant," added Tynan then, "was that going over people's heads would gain nothing. The answer would be the same all the way to the top. If I'd thought someone would reverse the decision, I'd have tried."

"That's it then," said Strong.

Jones looked at the men with him and demanded, "Why?"

Before Tynan could answer, the waitress was there asking if he wanted anything to eat. At first he was going to tell her that he only wanted coffee, but then decided to eat breakfast. French toast, orange juice and a glass of milk. The others ordered too and when the waitress disappeared, they sat quietly.

Then Jones asked, "Why do we have to give up now?"

Strong said, "Maybe because we have no authority, we have no plan and we have no way of crossing the ocean."

"Three very solid reasons," said Webster.

"No they're not," responded Jones. "They are three problems that we can handle, but they are not reasons for not pursuing this farther."

Tynan finished his water and said, "Two we could easily remedy. But the lack of authorization is the killer. There is no way to get around it."

"As private citizens," said Jones, "we could do something about it."

"No," said Tynan, "that's not true. There is a law that prohibits private citizens from engaging in activity that would be considered policy making, especially if that policy flies in the face of established governmental policy. And there is other legislation making it illegal to recruit mercenaries inside the United States to fight in foreign conflicts."

"But that's just plain stupid," said Jones.

"Makes no difference how you feel," said Tynan. "That is the law. We initiate a plan of high adventurism that takes place in a foreign nation, then we're in violation of the law and can be prosecuted."

"If they know who it was," said Jones.

"As long as they know," agreed Tynan.

The waitress returned and set glasses of juice in front of

everyone and then poured coffee for those who wanted it. She stood there for a second and then left.

"So that's it then," said Webster again.

"NO!" snapped Jones. "That's not it. Those assholes gunned down a SEAL."

Tynan grinned and lowered his voice. "This is classified right now and I shouldn't mention it, but it looks as if our SEAL took a couple of them with him. The report I heard was vague, but it seems he got his hands on a gun and opened fire, shooting several of them."

"All right," said Jones, clapping his hands. "That's what I wanted to hear."

The waitress reappeared and began handing out the food. When she finished, she asked, "Anything else?"

"More juice," said Tynan.

"Right."

"So," said Tynan, pouring syrup on his French toast. "After we eat, we head back to whatever we were doing."

"Skipper," said Jones. "I can't believe that you're giving up this easily."

"There is nothing more that can be done."

Jones wiped his mouth on his napkin and sat back in the booth. He stared at Tynan and then said, "We don't have to give up yet. We can look into this thing. What would happen if the terrorists suddenly died? Someone got in there, killed them and then got the hell out. No one would have to know who it was, except maybe potential terrorists in the future. A sneak and peek type raid, except that we kill the terrorists."

"It's not authorized," said Tynan patiently.

"Ignore that," said Jones. "Could we do it?"

Strong picked up the ball then. "Sure, we could do it, as long as we could get the equipment into place. We sure as hell couldn't check it as luggage."

"Why not?" asked Jones.

"Customs," said Tynan. "Even if they didn't look at this end, they would at the other."

"Then we could bribe the officials," said Jones.

"I wouldn't want to take that chance," said Tynan. "That could fall through. We could be double crossed. No, the weapons would have to go in another way."

Webster spoke up. "I know a couple of guys in the Air Force who are always flying to foreign nations. Transport pilots. We could get them to drop a cannister or two for us as a favor."

"Providing they are scheduled to the right place," Tynan reminded him.

"If they're not, they might know someone who is. Getting the weapons in wouldn't be that major of a problem."

"Okay," said Tynan. "How about this? We wouldn't want anything of US manufacture. Soviet AK's, maybe a Soviet-made Dragunov sniper rifle."

"Would we be bringing them back?" asked Strong.

"Hell no," said Tynan. "We'd have to leave them behind. No way to get them out."

"Complicates the problem," said Strong, "but I have access to an arsenal of Soviet weapons that we use for training. Everything we need is there, but I'm not sure how we'd cover their loss for an inspection."

"There any silencers in that arsenal of yours?" asked Jones.

"Everything we could need is in there. Silencers, flash and stun grenades, extra ammo. Problem is accounting for it if we lose some of it. ATF takes a dim view of automatic weapons and silencers disappearing, if they learn about it."

"We can work something out," said Tynan. "It's more of a paperwork problem than anything else." He picked up his juice and drank.

"I think the larger problem," said Webster, "is getting over there."

"That strikes me as the least of the problems," said

Jones. "We buy tickets and fly in just like any other tourist."

"Except there might be visa problems," said Tynan. "Some of these countries require that you apply for an entrance visa months in advance and there is no way to short circuit the machinery without using the State Department and we don't have access to that."

Jones picked up his orange juice and drank it. As he set the glass down, he asked, "How would you do this, Skipper?"

Tynan put down his fork and closed his eyes for a moment concentrating on the task. He opened them and said, "It presents an interesting problem. First is the weapons. If Strong can get them and Webster could arrange to have them flown overseas, we could coordinate a drop site so that we could pick them up. That's a minor problem."

The waitress came back again, gave Tynan his new glass of juice. As she left, Tynan said, "The real problems would be to get us into the country and to get us the information, the intelligence we need."

"What would be the classification level?" asked Strong.

"I'd expect it to be secret at the highest."

"Then that's no problem. I can get with the unit intelligence officer here and read the latest traffic. That's easy."

"If we can't get into Libya," said Webster, "maybe we could get into Egypt or Morocco or somewhere and sneak across the border."

"That would be better," said Tynan. "Couldn't trace us into Libya that way."

Jones grinned and asked, "So what more do we need?"

"How about permission?" said Tynan.

During the day, the terrorists roamed the aisles of the plane, swearing at the passengers, threatening them, striking one or two as the mood moved them, but did little else. One of them had finally untied Calhern's hands but she hadn't been allowed to rejoin the women and children in the rear of the plane. She was stuck up in the front with the young men and the bodies of the terrorists killed.

And since it was hot, the bodies stored up front were already beginning to stink. Not a light, almost unnoticeable odor, but a stench that seemed to roll out of the galley where they lay. It filled the cabin and threatened to make her and everyone else sick. But she didn't say a word to the terrorists. Now she was afraid of them.

One of the young men sitting up front with her finally leaned forward and asked, "Are you all right?"

She turned and looked into his eyes. Light blue eyes that were nearly washed out and invisible. He had a stubble of beard on his face and dark circles under his eyes. His hair was sweat damp, hanging down his face.

"I'm fine," she said. "Just fine."

She leaned back then so that she wouldn't have to talk to the man, afraid that the terrorists would hear and think they were conspiring. She wiped the sweat from her face. Her dress was soaked and she had already unfastened the top of it to see if that would cool her any. She'd pulled her hem up to her thighs and had struggled out of her panty-hose, but none of that helped. Not baking in the oven that the fuselage had become.

The terrorist leader had been sitting in the cockpit with the pilots. There had been shouting from there and a sudden wet slap followed by silence. The terrorist had exited and stood staring at the people in the first class cabin. The anger on his face was unmistakable. It looked as if he was going to drag two, three, all of them outside and shoot them in front of the assembled world press.

Then he pushed his way into the rear of the plane where he shouted at one of his companions in Arabic. There was a heated argument. Two men shouting, and then a woman screaming. Finally the leader said something and everyone fell silent.

A moment later the children began moving toward the front of the plane, lead by the female terrorist. They stopped at the door, milling there where the blood was thick and the flies were buzzing.

Several of the older women joined the children and then the terrorist leader pushed forward. Calhern was suddenly afraid that he was going to shoot the children to prove how serious he was. Gun them down on the ramp so that the world would see that he was a ruthless man who meant what he said.

Calhern stood up, blocking the aisle. "What is happening?" she asked.

"It is none of your concern."

She glanced toward the open door and said, quietly, "The children."

"They are being released to show our good intentions. We do not make war on children. They are innocent pawns for everyone in the world, and we are proving that we are not terrorists but fighters for freedom."

"Thank God."

The terrorist stared at her. "You had better sit down or you will be shot."

"Yes," she said. "Of course." She fell back into the seat and sighed.

The female terrorist walked out into the bright, afternoon sunlight. She stood at the top of the ramp, stained with blood that was covered with flies. She shouted something, gestured with the AK-47 she held, and the first of the children left the aircraft.

Calhern suddenly felt good. Maybe there was some hope for all of them after all. The terrorists were giving up some of the hostages and maybe more would follow later as another show of good will. The negotiators were trading something for the children and the old women. She didn't know what it was, but knew that it gave them all hope. As long as the two parties were talking, trading, dealing, there would be hope. Just so long as they didn't start shooting passengers again.

Suddenly the stench in the plane, the heat that had to have reached a hundred and thirty, the overflowing toilets, the lack of food and water, was tolerable. Anything was tolerable, if there was hope.

Tynan looked at the remains of his breakfast and said, "Webster will check with his Air Force connections to see if we can get the weapons delivered for us. Strong, you'll have to see if you can get the weapons and if there is a problem with accounting for them. You'll also have to secure the latest intelligence reports for us since you have the access to that. Jacobs, you'll need to find the other equipment we'll need. Radios, stun grenades, knives, flashlights, rations, and anything like that you think we might need. Jones, you'll have to check with the State Department and learn what you can about obtaining visas and I'll check the flight schedules, putting together an itinerary based on the best of the situations. Questions?"

As he searched the faces of the men, he realized that at some point the discussion had changed from whether to make the raid into a planning session for it. He'd never said he'd go along with it and suddenly, here he was giving the men instructions for it.

He was about to call it off when he realized that he wouldn't have to. The hijacking could be over already, or it could end in the next hour or two. It might be that they couldn't get some of the equipment arranged, or transport and visas wouldn't be available. There were a dozen ways the project could be stopped and Tynan didn't have to say a word. He'd let it go and see where it went. If nothing else, it was good training in the planning and execution of a covert operation organized outside ordinary channels.

"I suggest," he said finally, "that we meet at one o'clock this afternoon to see where we are." He looked at his watch. "That gives us something over three hours to see what we can learn."

Jones leaned over the table and lowered his voice. As he glanced into the faces of each of the men there with him, he asked, "We really going to go through with this?"

"Who knows?" asked Tynan. "We can put the wheels in motion and see what we can learn, but hell, if the hijackers release the passengers, then our mission is over."

"No sir," said Jones. "We still have to get even for killing the one man."

"That would be an easier task," said Tynan, "and would probably make the government happier, but let's just take it one step at a time."

"One o'clock then," said Strong. "Where?"

"Let's get a place a little less public," said Tynan. "I'll volunteer my hotel room if there are no objections."

"None, if you get us something to eat there."

"Christ, Jones, you just had a big breakfast and you're worried about lunch," said Jacobs.

"We'll work that out later," said Tynan. "Any important questions?"

There were none.

7

The men assembled in Tynan's hotel room with only Jones being late. He arrived ten minutes after the others and sat down on the floor. Tynan stood with his back to the window, the blinds drawn so that it was dark in the room. The television was on in case there were news updates on the situation in Libya.

Tynan looked at King who was standing by the door and asked, "You want to stay for this?"

She shook her head. "The less I know about it, the better I'm going to feel."

"Give us about two hours then," said Tynan.

When she closed the door on her way out, Jones said, "What about lunch?"

"That can wait." Tynan moved away from the window and pulled a chair closer. He put his foot in the seat and leaned an elbow on his knee. "Anyone come up against a wall that is going to stop us completely?"

When no one said anything, Tynan continued. "Looking at the map, I find that entrance into Egypt is prohibitive. We'd be twelve hundred miles or farther from the airport. We could spend three days trying to get there. Tunisia is probably our best bet, but that still leaves three or four hundred miles short."

"Couldn't we drop into the Mediterranean Sea and swim on in?" asked Jacobs.

"Who's going to let us bail out of their airplane over the ocean? Without official sanction, we're stuck," said Tynan. "If we can get into Tunisia then we might be able to work our way into Libya."

"What about the Israelis?" asked Jones. "They certainly wouldn't worry about national borders and expressions of neutrality."

"Let's not complicate this any more than we have to. Anyway, we can get into Tunisia fairly simply. Once there, we should be able to hire transport to get us to the destination. Flight arrangements can be made this afternoon but we'd have to leave here in about three hours."

"That's going to make it hard to secure the weapons," said Strong. "I can get them and they can get lost on a training exercise. No one's going to ask too many questions. But to get them here that fast. . . ."

"Get on the phone and arrange it."

"Before I do that," he said, "maybe I'd better give you the intell update on the situation."

Tynan moved around so that he could sit down. "Give us what you have."

Strong took a pad out of his pocket and grinned. "I know that I'm not supposed to take notes, but I wanted to get this right. The terrorist group responsible is the October the Twenty-seventh Faction. It operates independently and is suspected in a couple of car bombings and one assassination attempt. That's about all anyone knows about them."

"Shit," said Jones. "I could have gotten that off the television."

"Of course you could," said Strong calmly, "but what they don't know is the leader of the faction. That's a little bit of intelligence that is being guarded, but I have learned his name and we think that he operates out of Libya. His home is in Tripoli."

"Ah ha," said Tynan. "It begins to come together."

"Yes sir." He flipped the pages in his notebook and said,

"They've released some of the passengers as a good will gesture and they've been debriefed."

"You learn anything useful?" asked Webster.

Strong nodded. "First problem is an indication that the local military is supporting the terrorists. Passengers reported two to four terrorists until the plane landed and then more once they were on the ground. They were reinforced by the local military."

"That's going to fuck us up."

"More than a little," said Tynan.

"There are no official counts of the number of dead after a shootout on the plane, but apparently Chief Petty Officer Allen Pruit was able to grab a weapon and shot four or five of the terrorists and local military. Passengers reported two bodies on the plane."

"All right," shouted Jones. "Take some of the bastards with you."

"Knock it off," said Tynan.

"Anyway, to enter the aircraft, we're going to have to avoid the local military, and the passengers claim that the plane is surrounded by military vehicles. Pictures from the airport confirm that."

"Damn!" said Tynan.

"Passengers are split into two groups. The young men, those we'd have claimed were military age, are held in the front of the plane. The women, those who weren't released, and the older men are held at the rear of the coach class cabin."

"I can see one thing we need right now," said Tynan. "A diagram of the seven oh seven."

Strong continued. "Passengers said that there were between five and ten terrorists and military officers on the plane at all times. They were normally standing in the aisles or moving around while the passengers were seated."

"That's a break," said Tynan.

"Second break is that the military are all wearing khaki

as are the terrorists. Passengers are in normal civilian clothes."

"Okay, anything else?" asked Tynan.

"Only that the passengers were traded for some food and water, so the assumption is that the passengers have been fed. The passengers also mentioned that some of the passengers have been beaten and that it was getting incredibly hot in the plane. Interestingly, the terrorists haven't demanded fuel for a flight somewhere else. Libyan government is continuing to negotiate but there is no end in sight."

"Okay," said Tynan. "Now get on the phone and see if you can coordinate the weapons."

"Aye aye, sir."

"Jones, what can you tell me about the visas?"

Webster interrupted. "Sir, before we get into that, let me say something. I've talked to my Air Force friends, suggesting only in the vaguest sense what we had in mind."

"And?"

"They've offered their complete cooperation. Not only taking in the weapons pod, if that's what we want, but they'll take us too. We can bail out closer to the actual destination."

"Why didn't you say something in the beginning?"

"Wanted to hear the intelligence report. See if there was a chance that we could pull this off."

"Jones," said Tynan, "what did you learn about the visas?"

"Well, sir, they were going to be a problem because of a waiting period. Egypt was going to be our best bet, but hell, we don't need to worry about that now."

"Right," said Tynan. "Once we get into the country, we still have to get out through normal channels."

"Sir," said Webster, "once we've completed the mission, if we can get to an American base, or an airport used by our Air Force, we can get manifested out."

Tynan waved a hand. "Let's come back to that. Jacobs, you get the equipment?"

"Strong could get the flash grenades," he said. "The rest of the stuff, except the knives, I could buy almost anywhere. The knives, if you don't have one with you, can be purchased at a sports store. No problems."

Tynan opened the map and laid it on the table near him. He studied it for a few moments and then said, "I don't know about this."

Strong got off the phone and turned toward Tynan. He held up a thumb, grinning. They could get the weapons and the paper chase for them could be taken care of. That included the silenced pistols, the flash grenades, thermite grenades and a few timers for them. The last items were thrown in as afterthoughts. Tynan approved of them.

The sun set but the interior of the plane didn't seem to cool off much. During the day, after the women and children had been released, the rest of the hostages, including the cockpit flight crew, had been moved into the rear of the plane, away from the open door. Calhern welcomed the change in the environment, but it was no cooler in the back. The stench of the rotting dead was replaced by the stench from the overflowing and failing toilets.

But there was some relief. As soon as the children and the women were gone, a truck drove up. A huge yellow hose was attached and cool air was pumped through the plane for an hour. Water and food were also brought in and everyone was encouraged to eat and drink as much as possible.

Calhern was in a seat with two others. She could smell them now, along with the effervescence boiling from the stuffed toilets. She had nothing to say to the seatmates, a young man and a young woman. No one had much of anything to say to anyone. They were all beginning to wear down. The heat, the tension, the lack of adequate food and water were all beginning to take their tolls.

It was at dusk that the terrorist leader stepped through the curtain from the first class cabin and said, "I have announcement now. You will all listen to me carefully. Your very lives depend on it."

Calhern listened, but she was no longer interested in seeing the man. There was nothing about him that she didn't already know. She had studied him so that she could describe him to authorities after the ordeal ended.

"We have wired this aircraft with explosives. If anyone tries to storm it, we shall destroy the aircraft and everyone on it. We warn you because it is now your responsibility to ensure that we succeed in our mission."

The man then turned and disappeared. Only two of the terrorists remained in the cabin with them. The woman who stood with her back against the bulkhead so that she could stare at them, and one of the men sitting in the first seat by the curtain.

The thing that Calhern noticed was that no one reacted to the news that the plane would be destroyed. They accepted it with the same calm exteriors that Californians accepted the knowledge they were living on an earthquake fault. There was nothing they could do about it so they ignored it.

Calhern shifted around. Her body was beginning to rebel against the forced inactivity. She wanted to get up and walk. She wanted to breathe air that was fresh. She wanted a bath and a cold drink and the knowledge that she wasn't likely to die in the next ten hours.

"They'll come for us soon," the young man whispered to the young woman. "They'll come and free us and we can go home again."

She didn't respond to that but asked, "Do you really think they'd blow up the airplane?"

The man took her hand and whispered, "No. They'd kill

themselves too. It's a threat made just to keep us in line. Makes it easier to control us."

Calhern started to speak to them but then didn't. There was no reason to tell them that they'd better hope that no one came for them. There was no reason to tell them that the terrorists were fanatics who would be happy to die for their cause. There was no reason to tell them that a death in the fight would make the terrorists into instant martyrs with a direct path into heaven. And there was no reason to tell them that if the airplane blew up, they would all die.

She turned away from them and stared at the window although the shade was down. "Just get me out of here," she prayed silently. "Just get me out."

"Weapons are a go," said Strong.

"Equipment can be purchased and sorted within an hour," said Jacobs.

"Transportation in has been arranged," said Webster. "We show up at the embassy and say our passports were stolen, we should be able to buy airline tickets out."

"We can get an intell update at the airfield," said Strong. "And, if we take a good shortwave radio with us, we can keep up with the latest on the news."

Tynan rocked back in his chair and reviewed everything in his mind. It was one of those missions that was taking on a life of its own. A suggestion had been made, a few plans put into effect, and suddenly, the mission was on. It was coming together with the men stumbling into solutions that should have taken weeks to work out. Something had been eliminated.

And suddenly, Tynan wondered if it was the bureaucratic control that caused all the problems. Since they were operating outside the system, they didn't have to deal with the dozens of petty bureaucrats who had stop signs in their hands. The visas were short circuited and then suddenly bypassed. The forms that had to be signed to secure the weapons were no longer important. The weapons would be borrowed and if lost, written off. Transportation was ready and the ancillary equipment was available through outside sources.

"I can't see a problem," said Tynan.

"Parachutes?" said Jones.

"Hell," countered Webster, "we can pick those up at the Air Force base."

Tynan stood up, glanced at the TV screen and then shut off the set. "I think that before we continue on, we'd better make a couple of conscious decisions. Up to this point, we've let our enthusiasm carry us along without a look at the consequences of our actions."

"What are you getting at, Skipper?" asked Jones.

"Just this. We are not involved in a mission that is official. It is a mission that we've initiated on our own and planned on our own. There is no obligation on the part of anyone to follow it through."

"What do you intend to do, Skipper?" asked Jacobs.

Tynan glanced at the floor and then rubbed his chin. "Let me say this before I answer your question. We are about to embark on an illegal mission. We have no authorization and if we are caught, there is going to be no one to help us. If we're killed, we probably won't care. But the important thing to remember, if the enemy, if the Libyans arrest us, I doubt the State Department or the Navy will be thrilled with us. We won't be able to count on help from that corner."

"So," said Jones. "What's the point?"

"The point is, this is a mission that no one is required to go on. I'm not ordering anyone into the field. If you've all thought about it, and want to continue, then that is one thing, but if you want out, then bail out now."

"We understand that, Skipper," said Jones.

"Okay, then. I just thought everyone should have the chance to get out before we continued talking about this. I wanted everyone to take a moment to think about this before we left. Once we're on the plane, it'll be too late to get out."

"Yes sir," said Jacobs. "Just what are you going to do about this?"

"Shit," said Tynan. "I thought that was obvious. I haven't done anything too smart in the last few months. I don't know why this should be any different. I'm going."

8

Tynan found it impossible to relax in the rear of the C-130 Hercules. It wasn't a plush, comfortable civilian aircraft, but a stripped down military version with webbing strung along the fuselage for seats and no soundproofing on the inside. Heat blew down from the top and there was cold bleeding up from the bottom. Each change in the flaps was announced by a whine of the servos. The load master and flight engineer circulated in the rear, but didn't have much to say to Tynan and his men.

It had been a rush to get to the plane, manifested through so that they could board, and then someone had to lose the manifest. They had run across the tarmac and leaped into the rear of the aircraft. The pod with the weapons was already on board, strapped down, as were the parachutes. Tynan wasn't happy about that, but the timing had become so critical that it couldn't be helped.

Jacobs had gotten the hand held radios at Radio Shack. Tynan was worried about something called Space Cadet, but they had the appropriate range, they were reliable, and the speakers could be understood. Jacobs also had knives, boots, canteens, flashlights, and other such equipment.

The load master locked the equipment down and Tynan sat on the troopseat staring at it. As the pilots ran up the engines and made the final checks before takeoff, Tynan thought about his last moments with King.

She had understood what was happening. She knew why he thought they had to go, and what he planned to do. After the mess in Honduras, she understood that violence was sometimes the only way to solve some things, but she didn't understand why Tynan had to fly in the face of good sense and public policy.

With her sitting on the bed, looking up at him, he said, "Because there is no one else to do it."

"Surely the government must be in a better position to decide this."

"Stevie, I don't want to argue about it now. If I thought the government was going to react, I wouldn't go, but they have the attitude that if they debate, discuss and argue long enough the ordeal will solve itself."

"That doesn't mean you have to go."

Tynan nodded, as if to agree but said, "The problem is the terrorists shot a SEAL. That is something we just can't allow to happen."

King just shook her head. "I'm not going to visit you in jail. You go to jail and that's it."

"No one is going to jail." Tynan knelt and took her hand. "Do you understand?"

"Yes," she said. "That's the one thing that pisses me off most. I do understand."

They'd left it at that. She wasn't angry with him for going, although she thought it stupid that he would risk his career, and more importantly, risk his life. But then she did understand why he had to do it.

Tynan had gone and met with Jones. They'd taken a taxi to Bolling Air Force Base, found Webster in the Operations building, and waited for the others to join them.

Now, thirty minutes after takeoff, as they climbed to twenty-five thousand feet over the mid Atlantic, he was ready to review the operation again. He spread out the maps that he'd gotten from the Air Force. They showed the whole coast line of Libya, showed him all the population centers, but more importantly, showed him all the military installations. From the pilots, he'd gotten the approach plates and the airport guides for the airfield. That told him all that he needed to know about the airport.

Given what he knew, they'd want to approach from the southwest, cut holes in the chain link fence if it was in the way, and then try to approach the aircraft from its blind side. The open door was opposite them. From the news reports and the intell debriefings, he knew the shades were down. No one should see them coming.

The details continued to swirl around his mind. He would think of something, check it out, ask a question and then sit back again. This wasn't one of the well planned raids into North Vietnam, or a sanctioned excursion into South America. This was a haphazard raid into Libya thrown together by five men because a Navy man had been shot.

After an hour, Tynan called the men together. Jacobs and Jones had been using a whetstone to sharpen the new knives, Strong had been checking the weapons, and Webster had been in the cockpit, talking to the pilots.

Crouched around the maps and approach plates, Tynan had gone over the plan, such as it was. The major problem now, was to get on the ground in Libya. They'd moved from the DZ to the airport, trying to arrive about midnight. They'd need the darkness to cover their approach and to cover the infiltration. Once there, they would assess the situation, watching the military to see if they needed to worry about them. One man, probably Webster, would stay back with the Dragunov sniper rifle both to take out any of the terrorists who got out of the plane and to cover a retreat if needed.

They talked it out again and again. Tynan had each of the men brief the plan back to him. They tried to find holes in the plan and then tried to find solutions to them. They talked their way through all of it. They kept it simple so they could modify it in the field.

The load master stopped near them long enough to offer each of them something to drink. Tynan took a Coke, drained half of it and then rocked back, sitting on the deck near the equipment pod that was tied down.

Finally he stood up and moved toward the rear where he could look out of a porthole in the troop door. Far below was a deck of clouds and through it, he could see the ocean. As he studied it, he wondered if it wasn't too late to pack it in. They could stay with the aircraft and catch the turnaround back to the States. They didn't have to jump into the Libyan desert.

But then he remembered the news footage of the body lying under the fuselage of the jet. If nothing else, they had to get that body out of there. No one deserved to lie out on display like that.

Tynan turned and walked back to his seat, stepping carefully because of the rails on the deck of the plane. They were long bars with rollers in them that allowed heavy pallets filled with cargo to be dragged out the rear of the aircraft. One man could push a pallet with very little effort.

He sat down and checked the time. The flight was a long one with a stop in the Azores for refueling. A long flight with plenty of time to go over everything a second and then a third time.

For a moment he watched as Webster checked out the parachutes. Of all the problems, the one that worried Tynan the most was the parachutes. He'd have preferred packing his own, but the opportunity hadn't been there for it. They'd had to take chutes packed by an Air Force master rigger. He'd have to trust the man to have done the job right.

He leaned back into the red webbing and closed his eyes. It had been a long day, filled with a variety of activities. As he thought about it, he realized that he'd never actually made a decision to go on the mission. They'd started talking about how to do it and the next thing, he was on an airplane flying across the Atlantic.

The transportation had been simple. Every member of the active and reserve armed forces could use military air. Hell, veterans could fly on stand-by. If a plane was going to the destination you wanted, and there was space available, you could fly. Tynan knew that there were men who traveled the world using the space available route. That was basically what they were doing now. The difference was that the crew was going to let them bail out, which was not standard.

That worked only because Webster knew the crew and they understood what was happening. That was something else about the military. Everyone knew how to handle the terrorist problem. Everyone knew that ruthlessness was the only way to deal with it but the civilians who controlled the military and the government just couldn't see it. So, there were military men who'd bend the regulations a bit to help, if they thought the plan had the smallest chance of succeeding.

He dosed for a while. The sleep wasn't deep and he was vaguely aware of what was happening around him. Jacobs talking to Strong about the weapons. The sniper rifle hadn't been zeroed which meant it would be difficult to make a long shot accurately. The assault weapons, the AK's hadn't been zeroed either, but that wasn't as critical. The silenced twenty-twos had no stopping power.

He slept deeper and woke up as they landed in the Azores. Everyone had to get off the plane as it was re-fueled. Tynan and the boys stayed together in the VIP lounge drinking Cokes and eating the sandwiches supplied. Not the best food, but it was free and it was filling.

After he ate, Tynan went and found the aircraft commander who was in operations studying the weather for the next phase of the mission. He walked up to him and asked, "What are the chances of getting an intell update?"

The pilot glanced at his weather charts and shrugged. "I guess we could take a shot at it."

He walked over to the operation's clerk and said, "Can we get an intell briefing on the situation in Libya and the reaction in Egypt?"

"Yes sir. Intell office is across the hangar. Out the door, through the one on the other side and up the stairs. The NCO should be there."

"Thanks."

Together Tynan and the AC walked across the hangar floor. It was concrete that had been waxed until it had a smooth surface. There were yellow lines painted on it showing the safe places to walk and to help ground crews in marshalling the cargo and aircraft during deployments. They opened the door on the other end and climbed the stairs.

The intell office was marked with a sign which surprised Tynan. The intell function was one of those that wasn't supposed to be identified. You were supposed to have to ask for instructions.

The door wasn't locked. The sergeant, a young man in fatigues, sat with his feet propped on his desk, reading a *Time* magazine. When he saw the two officers, he dropped his feet to the floor and stood up. "Can I help you?"

"We're transitting the area and would like an intell update."

"Yes sir. May I see your ID card and a copy of your orders, please."

The AC handed the small green card to the NCO and then pulled a copy of his travel orders from his pocket. The sergeant studied them and nodded. "Okay." He looked at Tynan. "And you, sir?"

Tynan handed over his ID card and then gave the man a

copy of his leave papers. The document itself wasn't important, but it was a standard DoD form and on it was a space for a security clearance. Since Tynan was authorized to look at everything up to and including Top Secret, there was no problem.

"This way please."

The NCO led them into another room. There were file cabinets on one wall, three of them with combination locks on them. Once inside the office, the man asked, "What are you interested in seeing?"

"Latest traffic on the hijacking in Libya."

The NCO grinned. "You're in luck there. Got an update about twenty minutes ago." He stepped to one of the safes and began working the combination lock. He finished, pushed on the handle and then opened the top drawer. He fished a thick folder from it and handed it to Tynan. "That's everything we have. Latest data is on top."

"Thanks," said Tynan. He moved to one of the tables and sat down.

As he began to read, the AC asked for the latest available on any activity that would affect his mission. The NCO handed the pilot another folder and then said, "Not much going on in Egypt right now."

"Thanks."

The NCO then shut the drawer and locked it. He moved to the outer office, retrieved his magazine and returned. As he sat down, he said, "When you're finished, I'll take the folders. Please remember that the information in those reports is secret so please don't discuss them in non-secure areas."

Tynan read everything in his folder quickly and then went back and read the latest of the documents again, slowly. He wished that he could take notes, but that wasn't authorized.

Finally finished, he gave the reports back to the NCO and with the pilot, left the intell section. They returned to the operations side of the hangar. When they got there, they learned that the plane was ready for boarding again.

They were loaded back on the plane, strapped in and took off for the last leg. The plane was scheduled to land in Cairo, Egypt, but they'd drift off course slightly, putting them over land near Tripoli. The pilot and the navigator told him that they'd be embarrassed by making such a mistake, but they'd live it down.

As soon as they were at cruising altitude, Tynan moved to the center of the plane where the equipment was stored. He pulled out the maps again and then gathered the men around him. Again they went over the plan, discussing every aspect of it from the moment they left the plane until they walked into the American Embassy.

Finished with that, Tynan said, "I made a check on the latest information on the hijacking. Obviously, there has been no progress since we left. Terrorist demands have not changed and they're again threatening to shoot all the passengers. They haven't released any more people. Only good news is that the local military has pulled back. They still surround the plane, but they're four or five hundred yards from the aircraft itself."

"Why's that?" asked Jones.

"They had a bunch of reasons, but the intell analysis insists that several of their soldiers were killed and wounded in the shootout. Ambulances were seen racing to the aircraft after the firefight."

Jones clapped his hands once and said, "Old Pruit really did them in."

"More importantly," said Tynan, "he forced them back, giving us a better shot at the plane. He helped us out."

They talked about other things in the report, none of which affected the mission greatly. When he finished, Tynan leaned back on the stack of parachutes and said, "Anyone have anything that he wants to add to this?"

He surveyed the faces of the men with him. They stared back but no one said a word.

"Okay," he said, rubbing a hand over his face. "This is the point where the leader gives the pep talk to get you fired up for this, but damn, I don't know what to say. You all know exactly what we're doing and you all know the consequences."

"Yes sir," said Jacobs. "And we're not going to chicken out on you now."

The load master moved in and interrupted. "We're about forty minutes from your destination."

"Thanks," said Tynan. "Can you break out our equipment now?"

The load master unlocked the cargo straps that held everything in place. Once that was done, Tynan, with Jacobs' help, handed it out. They distributed the weapons and the ammo, the Radio Shack walkie-talkies, the freeze-dried rations, the canteens and the maps. Each man had his military ID card stuffed into the bottom of his left boot. Normally they would have left them behind, but they'd need the cards for identification to get them out of the country after the mission.

They struggled into the chutes and equipment, each man checking the others. They made sure that everything was ready to go, that all the straps were tightened down, that no one had forgotten anything. That finished, Tynan drilled them on the plan a last time. Planning was the thing that could wreck a mission as quickly as anything else, and yet he knew the old military saying: "When the first shot is fired, the plan is the first casualty." He sometimes wondered if the plan held together that long.

But then, good planning left them with options. A problem in the beginning wouldn't destroy them, just force them to improvise. Good planning gave them the ability to do that.

He stood there for a moment, looking into the faces of

each of the men, knowing that they couldn't go over the plan again. Everyone knew his job already. He didn't want them to get over ready.

"Any last questions?"

No one said a word. Jones smiled. It was a thin smile, his lips pressed together into a thin, white line.

"Worried?" asked Tynan.

"Only about the jump," said Jones. "I hate jumping out of a perfectly good airplane."

"No such thing as a perfectly good airplane," said Strong sarcastically.

"There is that," agreed Jones.

"Not worried about the mission?" asked Tynan.

"No sir. I know what has to be done down there. I fuck up and it's my fault. But I didn't pack this chute. Somebody else fucks up and it's my neck."

"Well, if it doesn't work," said Tynan, "you have my permission to punch out the rigger."

"Thanks, Skipper. I appreciate that."

"Anyone have a serious problem now?"

He glanced at each man in turn. Jacobs shook his head, as did Strong. Webster said, "No, Skipper." Jones stood there, lost in thought and finally said, "I guess not."

The load master returned and said, "We're about five minutes out. Pilot said that we're catching some radio traffic from Libyan flight control and flight following asking us who we are, but he's fucking with the radios. Making it seem we've some electrical problems."

"Thanks," said Tynan. He glanced at the men. "Let's get ready to go. When we get the green light, we go as quickly as possible."

"Aye aye, sir," said Jacobs.

9

Another day faded and there seemed to be no end in sight. The terrorists came and went, negotiating with the officials who had flown into the airport. Military men circulated through the aircraft, looking at the hostages almost as if they were animals in a zoo. They smiled at the women but they didn't speak. After a few minutes, another group would come through.

The sanitary facilities filled, overflowed and began to stink. The corpses of the men killed in the firefight the first day were rotting, the heat accelerating the decaying process. Flies filled the interior of the plane, their buzzing an annoying undercurrent to the rest of the misery.

Calhern had been allowed to stand in the aisle for five minutes and had been allowed into the restroom. The terrorists refused to let the women close the door and Calhern wasn't sure she could have stood being confined in the stinking, tiny room without the little circulation of air provided by the open door anyway.

At dusk, food was brought to the passengers, but again it wasn't very good. Stale bread, and meat that smelled as if it had lain in the sun. Fruits were provided, but Calhern stayed away from them. The stench rolling out of the rear of the aircraft was bad enough. The last thing they needed was for the passengers to get diarrhea.

There was plenty of water. The passengers were allowed to drink as much as they wanted. They could wash in it, bathing their faces and necks and trickling some on their chests. The relief was momentary, but in a world where there were no longer the smallest of pleasures, a little water to waste was a luxury of priceless quality.

The heat and misery that hounded them made the smallest task seem Herculean. Talking was no longer discouraged by the terrorists. They didn't have to. The passengers didn't have the energy or the desire to talk. They sat crammed into the rear of the jet, the heat sapping their strength, their energy, and waited for others to decide their fate by pushing the button to blow up the aircraft.

When Calhern believed that things could get no worse, when she believed that she would not live long if something was not done soon, and when despair hit the lowest level because she didn't know when the ordeal would end, it got worse. The chief terrorist pushed his way through the curtain that separated them from the front of the aircraft. He was flanked by two of his fellows, both dressed in khaki, their faces hidden by their kaffiyeh.

The leader stopped in the center of the aisle, an assault rifle held at port arms across his chest. He stared at the people, waiting for them to look up at him.

When he had their attention, he announced, "There has been a change in the negotiations. The governments of the world have decided to become difficult. They had decided that you people here, the innocent pawns in this continuing drama, are to be forfeit. They have announced that they will not waver from their rigid, chosen path which can only lead to your deaths in the very near future."

The men and women stuffed into the rear of the aircraft didn't respond. They had already learned that nothing they could say would do them any good. Their lives were held in the hands of men and women who didn't know them and didn't care if they lived or died. They sat quietly, waiting for the next piece of bad news.

"A deadline has been delivered. No longer do we talk of shooting one or two passengers to prove our sincerity. Such talk has fallen on deaf ears and the body of your fellow passenger, rotting on the hot tarmac under this aircraft, has not moved them to action."

Still the passengers sat quietly.

"I have told the various officials that this situation can not be tolerated. A solution must be found and found soon. To inspire them, I have given them until sunrise to satisfy our demands. If a satisfactory solution is not forthcoming, I will destroy this aircraft and everyone on it."

He didn't wait for a response to that news. He spun, shoved the curtains aside and disappeared. The two terrorists who had flanked him vanished with him.

Calhern sat, staring at the space vacated by the man. She was too numb to react. The threat of imminent death didn't scare her because she didn't believe it. She had knelt on the hot metal of the ramp up into the airplane and felt the muzzle of the pistol against the back of her head. Then she had been scared, but not panicked.

And now she wasn't even scared. Once you'd had the gun to your head, a verbal threat, no matter how menacing, no longer had the power to frighten it once might have held. The only thing she felt was an intense pain in her belly suggesting that she was about to get diarrhea and that was more frightening, at the moment, than the threat the plane would be blown up.

The C-130 Hercules had descended to fifteen thousand feet. When it reached that altitude, the load master had opened the troop door. He pulled on the handle, lifted in and then pushed up, shoving the door out of the way. A blast of fresh, cool air hit Tynan and his team in the face as they stood back, waiting for the word to go.

Tynan moved forward, to stand in the door. He glanced at the glowing red bulb that told him it wasn't time to jump. He looked out into the night and saw the Sahara stretching out into infinity looking like the calm surface of an ocean. Only a few points of light were visible to him. Oasis of light in the great sea of dark. The ground itself wasn't black like the jungle would have been. The sand reflected the light giving the ground a luminescence of its own. It wouldn't be like a night jump in Vietnam where the dangers were hidden in a shroud of black, but more like a jump at dusk. He would be able to easily see the ground and avoid anything dangerous.

"Getting close," shouted the load master over the roar of the engines and the wind.

Tynan moved up into the door. With his left hand he reached out and touched the side of the aircraft. He looked forward and saw the point where the land ended and the sea started far in front of him. And he saw a blossom of light, looking like a stain on a carpet. Ribbons of black extended from the stain, out, into the desert.

"Two minutes," said the load master.

Tynan turned and looked at Jacobs who was standing right behind him. They went through the ritual of checking each other's equipment one last time. Then Tynan turned and stepped up into the door where the wind was hitting him in the face and he could smell the stink from the engines as they worked to pull the plane through the air.

"Thirty seconds."

Tynan's gaze shifted from the scene outside, to the lights burning to his right. He stared at the red light, a dim bulb, barely visible to him in the darkened interior of the plane. Dim so that enemy gunners on the ground wouldn't be able to see it, if there were any enemy gunners.

"Fifteen seconds."

Tynan felt his stomach crawl and the hairs on the back of his neck bristle. Each time, he told himself that he wouldn't be scared and each time he got to the point of jumping without a thought about it. Then the clock began ticking and he thought about stepping off into darkened space and that scared him. He was sure that the chute would open. He was sure that the descent would be perfect. It was the jarring impact on landing that frightened him. He'd heard bones snap as men had hit wrong breaking their legs or arms or hips or backs. It was being too close to those men and hearing the bones crack that scared him now.

"Ten seconds."

Tynan took a deep breath and mentally rehearsed what he would do from the moment he stepped into space until he pulled the ripcord, to hitting the ground. Went through it slowly, thinking of each step, knowing that once he was out of the plane, it would all come naturally.

"Approaching the DZ."

Then the light went to green and the load master shouted, "Go. Go. Go."

Tynan stepped out of the C-130 and felt the propwash buffet him as he fell. He glanced up and saw the dark shapes of the men as they tumbled from the rear of the aircraft. Then he looked off, to the east, at the horizon, easily visible to him. He studied the city of lights off to his left, trying to orient himself with the map that he'd memorized. If the pilot had been right, then he was slightly southwest of the city. From there he could get himself to the airport in just a couple of hours of walking.

The noise from the C-130 receded in the distance. It was a shrinking black shape with light blue flames coming from the exhaust. Then the plane was gone and it was so quiet, he could have yelled up at the other men, giving them last minute instructions.

Finally, as he stared straight ahead, the horizon seeming to be almost at eye level, he pulled the ripcord. Behind him he heard the sound of the chute breaking free of the pack. There was a pop as the canopy deployed and a sharp, almost painful jerk as his descent was suddenly slowed. He looked up and saw the canopy filled with air, slowing him.

Near the ground, he put his feet together, flexed his knees and waited for the impact. He rolled with it, and then bounced up, onto his feet, pulled at the shroud lines to spill the last of the air held in the canopy. He ran forward rolling up the lines until he stood over the canopy. He hit the quick release on his chest and shrugged out of the harness.

Around him, he was aware of the others landing. Quiet sounds as the men rolled and then tried to get out of their chutes. Tynan crouched, and looked around. No one there but his men, all of them on the ground with no injuries.

Jacobs moved toward him and whispered, "Bury the chutes?"

"Of course. Not deep, but so that they're covered. By tomorrow at this time it won't matter."

Jacobs grabbed Tynan's chute and carried it to the pile being made. Webster and Strong were digging quickly while Jones ran a hundred yards to the east to provide some security. There was supposed to be a road in that direction and Jones was supposed to make sure that a car or truck driver hadn't seen them and stopped to investigate.

Tynan got out his map and then used his penlight, his fingers over the lense so that very little light escaped. He studied it, sure that they had landed right where they wanted to be, no more than five miles from the airport.

He looked up and then out over the city but there was nothing there except the hint of lights. He snapped off the penlight and then folded the map.

Jacobs reappeared and said, "We're ready. Wind might uncover the chutes tomorrow or bury them deeper."

"Doesn't matter," said Tynan. "Let's go."

He stood up and checked the safety on his weapon, making sure that it was on. Before he moved, he made sure that each of the others was there behind him and then started walking up the slight rise. The men strung out behind him. Unlike the jungle where they could move without disturbing the ground and leaving footprints, the desert was different. They couldn't move without making marks, but the shifting sands, driven by the light breeze, could fill in everything so that no one would be able to see the signs of their passing. Besides, by morning, it wouldn't be important.

They reached the top of the rise and scrambled over it, sliding down the other side. As they did, the whole scene was spread out in front of them like a relief map in a big city museum. The lights of the city highlighted the features so that Tynan could tell exactly where the airport was and could see the quickest route to it. There was no longer a question of whether they were in the right place or not. He could see easily that they were.

They kept moving, down to the bottom of the sand where the ground was firmer and it was easier to walk. The men followed along, staying on the firm ground, able to walk faster. They tried to make no noise.

Tynan was surprised by the weather. He'd thought it was going to be hotter, like walking into the blast furnace atmosphere around Las Vegas, but then realized that the sun wasn't up. The sun was what made the heat around Vegas almost impossible to take. The evenings, while hot and dry, weren't as deadly as the days.

After thirty minutes, he stopped to check the map again, although he could still see his destination in the distance. He drank some of the water in his canteen. And then stayed crouched on one knee. Sweat blossomed and dripped. He could feel it for a moment and then it was gone, evaporating in the dryness of the surrounding air.

Unlike Las Vegas, here, he could smell the ocean. He could tell they were close to the coast, the odor of salt and fish drifting on the breeze.

They started off again, winding their way along the valley floor, using it to cover their movements. They heard traffic on a road and once a flash of lights caused them to take cover. When the truck was gone, moving to the right along a road that was barely visible in the sand, they began again.

They came to one major road. A concrete highway that looked impossible to cross. The traffic, though sparse, seemed to be coming constantly. As soon as it looked as if it would be possible, another vehicle would appear.

Tynan slid along the road, moving more or less in the direction of the airport. They came to a low place where the road dipped down in what Jacobs described as a Texas bridge. The water, when and if it rained, was channeled along the arroyo and the road dipped down to ford it. Most of the time it was dry and there was no reason to build a real bridge.

But it provided cover for them. A truck or car would have to nearly be on them to spot them. With Strong and Jones stationed up on the sides where they could hide and watch the road, Tynan waited for their signal.

"Go," said Jones.

Tynan, bending low like he was trying to avoid the spinning blades of a helicopter, ran across the road. Once across, he threw himself onto the sand and waited. When Jacobs joined him a moment later, they took up positions to watch the road. A few minutes after that, the problem was solved and the men began the trip again.

Without another rest, they kept moving. The later it got, the fewer people they heard and the fewer vehicles were out. They kept the pace brisk until they came to the last obstacle. Tynan climbed it, stretched out on the sand and crawled the last few feet to the top of the dune. Some brush grew near the top, providing a little cover.

Before he reached the top, he took out his binoculars and then slipped forward. The lights on the airfield had been cut back so that there wasn't much to give it away. Through the binoculars he could see the chain link fence, the approach lights to one of the runways, an open area that led to a larger, built up area of hangars and other structures, and a tall building in the center of it. Through the binoculars it was unmistakable. The control tower looked like the control tower on any airport in the world.

Tynan swung to the right and spotted the lone jet sitting at the end of the runway. There were military vehicles parked around it and he could see little movement there, indicating that the Libyans were all asleep, as he'd hoped they would be.

He couldn't see much detail, given the darkness. The ideal situation would be to study the scene in the daylight and make the approach the following night. Daylight would reveal much that he couldn't see now, and it might give him a chance to count the number of Libyan military men around the plane.

There didn't seem to be any movement near the aircraft. It was dark except for a single spotlight on the door near the cockpit on the left side of the plane. That light could be a problem for them. One man, Webster, with his sniper rifle could take it out. Or maybe one of the assault team could do it. Before they hit the aircraft, they'd have to extinguish it.

The terrain around the runway seemed to be rough enough to hide them as they began their approach. There were arroyos and gullies and ditches that would conceal their movements until they reached the runway. After that it was going to be difficult to get to the door of the plane.

Studying the ground, he could see a way to penetrate the circle of military vehicles. Since no one would be worried about someone coming in from the outside, they would probably be watching the airplane. Tynan could see that his men could crawl almost to the edge of the runway without being seen by anyone there. Then, if the searchlight went out, they could probably get into the aircraft.

Jones joined him on the top of the dune and leaned

close, his lips nearly touching Tynan's ear. "Well, Skipper, what do you think?"

Tynan kept his eyes on the jet, looking for some sign that the people were still alive on the inside of it. He whispered, his voice so low that it was nearly blown away on the breeze, "This is going to be a tough nut to crack."

"At least it's isolated from the rest of the airport," said Jones.

"And we don't have to worry about the news media with its cameras," added Tynan. "Looks like everyone is being held way back from the plane."

"So what are we going to do?"

Tynan lowered his binoculars and stared at the man next to him. Then he glanced at the plane and said, "We're going to go free the hostages and punch out. Let the hostages run into the arms of the Libyan military and hope in the confusion we can get out."

"That going to work?"

"I sure as hell hope so because I'm afraid I don't have much more in the way of a plan." He picked up the binoculars and looked through them. Under his breath he said, "It sure as hell has to work."

10

Tynan crawled to the rear, keeping his eyes on the scene below him until the top of the dune got in the way. Then he slid down the sand. At the bottom he stopped, waiting for the rest of the team to join him.

"One searchlight," he said quietly, "set about fifty to seventy-five yards away, shining on the hatch leading into the jet. That's our first target."

When no one spoke, he pointed at Strong and said, "You'll take it out with one of the silenced pistols. One round into it should break the glass and the vacuum, letting air in to burn the filaments. That doesn't work, put a couple of rounds into it. Do you have one of the silenced twenty-twos?"

"Yes."

Tynan looked at the other men. Dim outlines against the light sand. "Once the light is out, we assault the jet. Up the steps and into it. Jacobs, you and Jones are first with the stun grenades and then the lights. I'll follow with one of the automatic weapons. Everyone in khaki goes down."

"What'll we do with the passengers?"

"Order the pilots and the stewardesses to get them out the emergency exits as quickly as they possibly can. We retreat the way we came. Strong, after you put out the light, you move up to cover our back."

"Aye aye, sir."

Tynan glanced at his watch. It was now nearly two in the morning. They'd have to hurry if they wanted to be in place by three. Two minutes for the raid and then two hours of dark to get clear.

"Questions?"

"What about Libyan soldiers?" asked Jacobs.

For Tynan, it was a damned irritating question too. Although the intelligence reports had suggested that the Libyans had welcomed the hijackers and had reinforced them, they were still the soldiers of a foreign nation that was not currently engaged in hostilities with the United States. It was a sticky damned question.

But then, Tynan knew there was only one answer. "Kill them if they get in the way."

"Aye aye," said Jacobs.

"Webster, you're on the top of the dune with the sniper rifle to cover the retreat. Anyone chases us, you drop him. I don't care who it is."

"Aye aye."

Tynan looked around the small group of men. "Anyone have anything else we need to talk about?"

Jones said, "No sir," for the group.

"I now have zero one one five."

The others adjusted their watches as Tynan counted down to the mark. "Strong, you have thirty minutes to get into place. You put out the light at zero one four five. We move the moment the light is out."

"Aye aye."

"If there is nothing else, then let's do it. Good luck and we rendezvous back here."

With that, Tynan stood up and turned. He worked his way along the side of the dune, staying low. When he could see the airfield, he got down to his belly and began to crawl toward a ditch to the right. He dropped into it, carefully and then got up to his knees. A moment later Jacobs and then Jones joined him. Strong moved off to the left, working in that direction so that he would be in a position to take out the light.

Now Tynan was on his feet again. He bent low, staying below the top of the ditch, following its rocky and broken path. He moved carefully, the only sound a quiet scrape of his boots in the sand. Although he still couldn't see the field without standing, he could see the glow of the lights.

Once he glanced back and saw that both Jacobs and Jones were there, moving with him. Shadows against the tan dirt and sand of the side of the arroyo.

He came to the end of it. A deep crevice that led from one side of the runway down to the desert. The chain link fence was stretched across the end of the arroyo, the bottom of it more than four feet from the ground. Sitting there, he could see the vehicles of the Libyan army silhouetted against the brightness of the spotlight to the west of them. There was no movement from the Libyans.

There was some scrub brush from the edge of the runway, out into the desert. From the end of the runway, leading along the approach path were a series of towers that held the approach lights to guide the planes. Although there were platforms at the base of the lights, there were no Libyans in them. Tynan wondered why, but then realized that the Libyans, like the hijackers, would be expecting nothing from outside.

Sitting there, he realized that they were going to have to sprint across the runway, to the stairs that led up into the plane. With luck, everyone would be looking toward the searchlight, wondering why it was out. Their eyes wouldn't be adjusted to the darkness. Then it would be too late.

Again Tynan looked at his watch. Strong had to be getting into position now. It was only a few minutes before the attack was to begin.

And then, coming out of the scrub to the right, from where the nose of the airplane was pointed, was a shape. A single soldier, his rifle slung over his shoulder. Tynan touched the silenced pistol on his belt and realized that it wouldn't be the right weapon. A twenty-two didn't have the stopping power of the larger caliber weapons. It was used because it was the most effectively silenced. But a shot, off by an inch, could leave the man alive to shout a warning. Hell, Tynan knew of an instant where the twenty-two slug bounced off the thick bone of the victim's forehead. Silencing reduced the muzzle velocity even more.

Carefully, he leaned his rifle against the wall of the arroyo, and pulled his knife. Moving slowly, he slipped to the other side of the ditch so that the man coming at them wouldn't see him. He ducked down, his face turned away as he listened to the footsteps of the man.

When he was closer, Tynan turned and saw him. Like the phantoms in a horror film, Tynan came up, out of the ground and grabbed the man from behind. Before the man could scream or fight or run, Tynan seized his chin, pulling upward to keep the mouth shut and the nose pinched off. Dragging the man back, down into the ditch, Tynan slashed with the knife. The sharp blade sliced through the delicate flesh. The soldier threw out his hands, as if praying, and his feet drummed in the loose sand. He groaned, low in his throat, but the sound wasn't very loud and didn't last very long.

As the man hit the ground on his back, the blood bubbling from the slash in his neck, Tynan struck again. He pushed the blade up under the breastbone to puncture the heart. Blood pumped from the chest, staining the khaki fabric dark red and filling the air with the smell of copper. A moment later the man spasmed and died and a new smell erupted.

"One minute," said Jacobs as he handed Tynan's rifle to him. "One minute."

*   *   *

Strong crawled along the ground, staying outside the pattern of light laid down by the Libyans. He used the shadows, the scrub brush and the depressions in the sand, moving slowly, carefully, rhythmically. One hand, then one foot, and then the other hand and foot. He pushed himself along, grabbing handfuls of sand, his eyes locked on the Libyan military vehicles parked around the plane.

He didn't have to get close to the searchlight. In fact, the farther from it he was, the better off he'd be. But shooting into a light wasn't the simple thing that everyone thought it was. It was difficult to aim, especially since he couldn't stand or sit. He had to remain on the ground. The only thing he had going for him was the fact that the light was so big. He didn't have to hit it dead center. He just had to break the glass so the oxygen could get in and cause the filament to burn.

He reached a point where he could see the searchlight easily under the belly of the plane. He was lying in a shadow created by the fuselage. A long, black area covered with scrub and filled with shallow depressions. The perfect place because an enemy soldier, a terrorist, a Libyan would have to trip over him to see him.

He shifted around so that he was facing the plane. He pulled the camo band off the face of his watch and stared at the numbers. Only a few minutes from the time he was supposed to put out the light.

Reaching up under the fatigue jacket, he pulled the silenced twenty-two free and worked the slide, making sure that a round was chambered. As he stretched out, he realized that on TV he'd have a revolver, probably something huge that would cough quietly when he fired it. Someone should explain to Hollywood script writers that the noise escaped from the end of the cylinder. Revolvers couldn't be silenced effectively. The pros knew it. The men who worked with weapons knew it. Too bad that the writers didn't.

Again he glanced at his watch, saw there were only a few seconds left. He stretched his arms out in front of him, bracing his elbows and keeping both eyes open. Closing one and using the sights just didn't seem to be right.

He squeezed the trigger. A slow, steady pull. There was almost no sound from the weapon other than the smooth working bolt as it ejected the spent cartridge and chambered a live round.

Strong was sure that he had missed. He didn't see how he could have, but the light still burned, brighter than ever. He aimed again as the light began to blaze brighter than the noonday sun. There was a blinding flash and sudden darkness. Shouting erupted as the Libyans yelled at one another.

As the light went out, Strong was on his feet running through the sand and then across the tarmac.

Tynan watched the last seconds tick off and whispered, "It's time."

But the light didn't go out.

Under his breath, Tynan said, "Come on."

And then the light brightened, flared, and vanished. As it did, he was up and moving. He ran at the nose of the airplane, hunched over, his rifle cradled in both his hands. Behind him he could hear both Jacobs and Jones.

When he reached the plane, he saw a shape there. A small man, dressed in khaki and holding an AK-47. Tynan didn't hesitate. He swung the butt of his own AK around, smashing it into the face of the Libyan soldier. He heard the bones snap as the man slipped to the ground. He dropped his weapon with a clatter.

Tynan dropped to one knee, watching the Libyan vehicles, but there was no movement there. Apparently no one had heard the falling weapon. Jones ran past him and up, stopping at the doorway. Jacobs then ran up the steps and moved to the door. As he did, Tynan left his post, followed them and then tossed a flash grenade into the aircraft. When it detonated, both Jones and Jacobs entered with Tynan right behind them.

In the light flashed around by Jones, Tynan could see no evidence that there was anyone in the front part of the plane. He was aware of the stench from the body that had baked in the galley all day.

The curtains at the far end parted and Tynan fired a burst from his weapon at the movement. The muzzle flashes strobed, almost touching the chest of the terrorist. He fell back, blood staining his shirt.

Screams erupted from the rear of the plane. Jones leaped to the bulkhead that separated the two cabins and threw a flash grenade into the rear cabin. As he turned his head, the grenade detonated in a roar that was louder than thunder and a flash that was brighter than lightning.

Jacobs pushed through, dived to one side and used his light. Tynan was right behind him. A man was moving up the aisle and Tynan cut him down. There was screaming from all around him. Shouts and orders. Jones entered, his light on and Tynan saw a khaki clad figure to the left, near them.

He opened fire from the hip. The figure was thrown back, against the seats, losing the weapon. It slipped to the floor as another man moved. Tynan fired again and the man disappeared between the seats. His weapon in the aisle.

"American sailors," Tynan yelled. "American sailors."

Jones and Jacobs were searching for more of the terrorists, but there didn't seem to be any of them left in the aircraft.

Strong reached the foot of the ladder just as the first of the flash grenades exploded. He had ducked under the fuselage as Tynan had run up the steps. As that happened, he dropped to one knee, watching the Libyans swarm over their military vehicles, but make no move to the jet.

There was a noise to his right and he turned. A fist struck him and he fell back, against the metal of the stairs. A shape loomed and fired, the flash of light illuminating his face. Strong lost the grip on his AK. As a flare of pain burst in his chest, he tried to draw the silenced pistol.

He slipped to the ground as the man stood over him, the weapon pointed down, at his face. There was an explosion at the end of the barrel and Strong felt a burning deep in the center of his chest. He tried to raise his own weapon, but didn't have the strength.

Strong collapsed as the man whirled and started to run. Strong tried to squeeze off a shot, but no longer had the strength to pull the trigger. The pistol fell from his hand, hitting the tarmac.

He tried to sit up, but couldn't. His body turned cold, as if winter had suddenly arrived in the desert. Things were confusing, impossible to figure out. He fell back, his head striking the tarmac and bouncing once. He wasn't aware that it had happened.

As the stars faded from sight, the night turning as black as the pits of hell, he wondered what had happened.

Stephanie King sat up watching a movie on television. It wasn't a particularly good movie, but it occupied the time and filled her mind. It kept her from thinking about Libya, hijackers, and where Mark Tynan had gotten.

The news bulletin destroyed the little peace of mind that she had. The Special Report sign flashed and then faded. On the screen she could barely see the shape of a jet plane. A dark, forboding shape.

"We do not know what has happened," the breathless commentator was saying.

King sat upright and then leaped from the bed. She twisted the volume knob.

"The searchlight that had been shining on the aircraft

since sunset suddenly went out. We're too far away to see much in the dark, but there seems to have been some shooting . . ."

The scene on the TV shifted to the interior of a building. Bright lights with dozens of people standing around, most of them looking tired. A man shoved a microphone at a Libyan officer who had appeared in the door.

He said something in French and then another man repeated it, speaking rapidly in English, "We do not know what is happening. The activity is not the result of any orders given our troops."

A siren went off then almost wiping out the voices. The camera shifted back to the newsman. He held the microphone under his mouth.

"We do not know what is happening, although the Libyans deny all knowledge of the activity. Speculation is that the hijackers are attempting to move the aircraft, though there are no indications that they have started the engines."

Again the scene shifted, back to the tarmac. Someone had turned on the airport lights so that the plane was easier to see, but still almost invisible. There seemed to be shapes running around it. Libyan soldiers, or terrorists. No one seemed to know and no one wanted to speculate.

King moved back from the TV and sat on the bed. She was hunched over, as if her stomach hurt. Her eyes were glued to the screen as the drama unfolded, though no one seemed to know what it showed.

"There are reports of shooting at the aircraft. Gunfire has been heard. The Libyans are denying that they have assaulted the aircraft, though none of the terrorists are in the terminal building now. There are reports that the negotiations were taking place here earlier today."

"Christ," said King. "You assholes don't know a thing. Why don't you shut up?"

But they didn't. The cameras still played on the aircraft

as the rear seemed to burst open. Cars, red and blue lights on them flashing, rushed out toward the aircraft.

"Christ," said King again. "What's happening?"

Tynan found himself crouching in the aisle, waiting for the counterattack. He kept his eyes moving, but everyone remained seated.

Finally one man stood up, his hands raised slightly. "The plane is wired."

"What?"

"Terrorists said that it was wired with explosives," said the man.

Tynan looked at the bodies, riddled with AK rounds. They weren't going to cause trouble. He didn't think the explosives would be radio command detonated. Not on an airfield where there were hundreds of radios. Someone in the plane would have to push the button and the enemy in the plane was dead.

Then a voice asked, "Are you really Americans?"

Tynan stood up. "Yes. American sailors. Where is the flight crew?"

A woman in a blue uniform stood and said, "Here."

"Get these people out of here," said Tynan. He had to get the people out of the plane as fast as possible, just in case there were explosives wired to it. "Out the emergency exits and run for the terminal. Get away from the aircraft as quickly as you can."

"But . . ."

"Do it," yelled Tynan. "Now!"

The interior of the aircraft erupted into cheering. The people were shouting, screaming, laughing as the stewardesses tried to get the emergency exits opened.

"Skipper," said Jacobs. "There was shooting behind us."

"I heard it."

A woman came at them. She held both her hands high,

as if she was surrendering to them. A tall, slender woman who looked as if she hadn't slept in days.

"Name's Calhern," she said. "Thank you."

"Please go with the others," said Tynan.

"Yes," she said.

Behind her the passengers were filling the aisles as the stewardesses worked to get them out of the plane. She turned back and said, "You didn't get them all."

"How do you know?" asked Tynan.

"The leader wasn't here. He didn't spend much time here," said Calhern. "A Libyan officer escorted him everywhere."

"Shit," said Tynan. "Not much we can do about that."

"Skipper, we've got to get out now too."

"Get the leader," said Calhern.

"Yeah," said Tynan. "We want him too. We may just have to settle for what we got."

"No," she said. "Get him and kill him."

"Skipper!"

"Right," said Tynan. He turned then, following Jones and Jacobs to the front of the aircraft as the passengers used the emergency chutes to get out and scatter along the runway, complicating the job of the Libyans. They could no longer tell who was who in the dark.

11

Jacobs leaped through the door, knelt at the top of the ramp and surveyed the scene. Tynan followed him and ran to the bottom of the steps. He turned to the rear where the people were exiting the aircraft. There were two or three at the bottom of each of the emergency exit chutes, helping those still in the aircraft to get out. Once a passenger hit the ground, he or she took off running. Around the rear of the jet and toward the terminal that was now alive with light. There were sirens wailing, lights were flashing and men were shouting. It was just the confusion that Tynan had hoped there would be.

Jones ran down the steps, stumbled and caught himself by grabbing the metal rail.

"Where's Strong?"

Tynan shrugged. Libyan soldiers were running along their line of vehicles, but none of them had broken away yet. "I don't know."

Jacobs came down, and stopped as three soldiers ran across the tarmac.

"Skipper?"

Tynan stood, his feet braced and his knees locked. He aimed carefully, the AK pressed against his shoulder. He didn't use the sights, but looked along the barrel. He squeezed the trigger and the men went down, sprawling.

From the Libyan lines, there was screaming, orders

shouted but not obeyed. Headlights came on, but the jeeps and trucks were pointed in the wrong direction. Passengers threw themselves to the ground screaming. Men were shouting as the Libyans tried to find cover. The shooting stopped as quickly as it had started.

"Found him!" yelled Jones.

Tynan back away from the steps, moving toward the aircraft. He watched the Libyans, afraid they would open fire on the passengers.

"Skipper, Strong's hit."

Tynan knelt and glanced to the right. In the light now coming from everywhere, he could see the ragged stain on Strong's uniform and the pool of black that had spread out around his body.

"Strong's dead."

"To the right!"

Tynan stood and turned. A soldier loomed out of the gloom, his head down, his weapon held in front of him. Tynan used the butt of his rifle to snap the barrel of the enemy's weapon out of the way. He continued the motion, putting his weight behind it, striking the man in the side of the head. The Libyan collapsed with a groan.

"Grab Strong," ordered Tynan.

Jacobs snagged an arm. Jones did the same, lifting the body partially off the tarmac.

"Go!"

As the two men began running, dragging Strong, Tynan picked up the AK-47. He slung the weapon and then turned so that he could watch the Libyans. They were swarming out onto the runway now, weapons pointed at the passengers. Cars, trucks, fire engines were racing along the runway, their lights illuminating the scene.

Tynan glanced over his shoulder and saw that Jacobs and Jones had dropped down into the arroyo, disappearing from sight. He turned, and sprinted after them. He leaped

and landed in the bottom of the sand choked arroyo. Jacobs
and Jones were there, waiting.

"Now what?"

"We get the fuck out of here," said Tynan.

"With Strong?" asked Jones.

Tynan looked over the lip of the arroyo, at the massed
confusion on the tarmac. There were hundreds of people
there now. News camera crews were roaming among the
freed passengers, their lights on the faces of those just
freed. Libyan soldiers and officers tried to find out what
had happened. They swarmed around the bodies of their
men and a few pointed into the desert, but no one followed. They were waiting for someone to give them orders
now.

There was shouting as everyone tried to get everyone
else's attention. Jeep and truck engines roared along with
the continued wail of sirens, some from the vehicles and
one klaxon from the terminal area.

"We take Strong. Get going. I'll cover."

Jones and Jacobs again grabbed the body and began
dragging it along the ditch, using the available cover.
Tynan remained at the front of the arroyo, watching the
airfield. No signs of an active pursuit developed.

Satisfied that they had gotten clear of the runway without the Libyans seeing them, he left his post. He ran down
the arroyo, came to a bend in it and stopped there. Still,
there was no pursuit.

The runway was filled with vehicles now. Ambulances
were racing toward the jet. The level of noise rose until it
was a roar that drowned out everything around it. People
were still running around, but no one was coming toward
them. The Libyans were trying to round up the passengers
who had scattered over the airfield. A group of soldiers
was finally trying to board the plane, working their way up
the steps, silhouetted in the bright lights from everywhere.

Behind him, Jones and Jacobs had reached the end of the arroyo and were up and out of it. They dragged Strong around the end of the dune and released the body. Tynan followed them, dropping to the soft sand there.

For a moment he rested, the excitement of the fight and the chase still bubbling through him. He wanted to run or shout but did neither. He gulped in the warm, dry desert air and tried to calm himself. Then he scrambled up the sand dune to where Webster still watched the scene.

"In and out," said Tynan softly.

Webster looked at him and said, "Saw Strong get it. Man came up on his blind side."

"What?"

"I think one of the terrorists stumbled in. Shot Strong and then got out."

"You see where he went?"

Webster nodded, his eye still to the scope of the Bragunov sniper rifle. "Better than that. I put a round into him."

"He down?"

"And then back up. Moved toward me then off to the south. I think I know where he went."

"Then let's go get him."

"I was hoping you'd say that."

Tynan slipped to the rear, down the back of the dune. Jones was going through Strong's pockets, taking everything that could identify him. He pulled off his boot to retrieve Strong's ID card. Jones stood up then and used the butt of his rifle to smash Strong's teeth. Tynan heard the crunch of bone and felt chills up his spine. He wanted to shout at Jones, but knew it had to be done. They didn't want the Libyans to be able to identify the body.

Jones slammed the butt into Strong's face again. Bone snapped and splattered. Tynan turned away so that he couldn't watch.

Jacobs joined him and asked, "What now?"

"We're going after the bastard who shot Strong."

"Good."

Calhern, after sliding down the emergency chute had turned to look back at the aircraft. She stood there, staring up at it and decided that she was never going to travel abroad again. Once she was safely in the United States, she was going to stay there, taking the train, bus or car if she wanted to go anywhere. If wanderlust set in, she could drive the Pan American Highway or arrange for a cruise to South America. Airplanes were out.

Then sirens started to wail and lights began to flash. There was gunfire and she was afraid that she had survived the ordeal on the plane to be gunned down just moments from rescue. She ducked under the plane and took off running toward the terminal, away from the Libyan army, and away from the shooting.

She stumbled and fell headlong into the soft sand. She lay there, her heart hammering and the blood rushing in her ears. She lifted her head and saw the cars and trucks rushing toward the aircraft. Instead of getting to her feet and returning to the jet, she dropped her head to her arms and relaxed.

With the odor of the sand in her nostrils, and with the sweat of excitement dripping, she thought of the ordeal. Terrorists threatening to kill her. Terrorists killing one of the passengers, threatening to blow up the plane, and then freedom by a group of American commandos. Men whom she never actually saw, other than dark shapes in the aisle of the aircraft.

As she lay there, she realized that the raid was unauthorized. That was obvious. If it had been sanctioned by the Libyans and the American government, the ambulances would have been standing by, not reacting five minutes late.

She rolled over and sat up. Around her were a few of the other passengers, standing or sitting on the sand, watching the scene at the runway like they were the audience in a theater watching a movie.

More people were arriving at the jet. Hundreds of them. Klieg lights for TV cameras were turned on, and if the news media was there, it was safe to return. Probably safer than lying in the sand where there were snakes and scorpions and probably a hundred other disgusting things.

She got to her feet and walked back toward the aircraft. As she reached the runway, a woman ran at her holding out a blanket to wrap around her shoulders.

Calhern smiled at that. Wrap the survivors in blankets, even when the outside air temperature is in the high eighties and everyone is sweating. She accepted the blanket, though, glad to have it.

A news man ran at her, his microphone held out like the baton to be handed over in a relay race. A cameraman trailed along behind, the minicam on his shoulder while a third man carried a bar of lights.

When he was still ten feet away, he shouted, "Can you tell me what happened?"

"We were hijacked," said Calhern.

"No, I mean just now. What happened on board the aircraft? How did you get away?"

"Down the emergency chutes."

"No," snapped the reporter. "What happened just prior to your using the chutes?"

Calhern drew the blanket around her as if she was suddenly cold. She stared into the intense face of the young man as he waited for an answer.

When she didn't speak right away, he said, "We have

unconfirmed reports that Americans boarded the plane and shot the terrorists."

"No," she said suddenly. "They weren't Americans. Israelis. I'm sure they were Israeli."

The man gestured at some of the other passengers and said, "They told us that the men announced themselves as American sailors."

"No," said Calhern. "I'm sure they said they were Israeli. I don't know why the others would say they were Americans."

"Then what happened?" asked the man, frustrated.

"Please," said Calhern. "It's been quite an ordeal. I'd like to see the doctor."

"Just one more question," said the reporter. "Do you know the name of the man killed?"

"I really want to see the doctor," said Calhern as she pushed passed the reporter. As she headed toward one of the ambulances, she heard the man say, "American commandos moments ago freed the passengers of the hijacked jet. American officials on the scene are denying all knowledge of the raid . . ."

"It would be my guess," said Tynan, "that if the hijacker ran off in that direction he either has a hiding place arranged, or has a vehicle parked."

"If he's got a car," said Jones, "then we're fucked."

Tynan glanced at the airfield and said, "In all that confusion, I'd bet you could drive off in a jeep and no one would be the wiser."

"Why me?"

"Because you're the best car thief I know. If there isn't just an ignition switch like in ours, then you could probably hot wire it."

"Don't I get a back up?" asked Jones.

"Hell, if it's going to be that big a deal, just slip away.

If worse comes to worst, we'll just get the hell out of here before we get fucked up."

"What about Strong's body?"

"Set a termite grenade under it with the pin pulled. Somebody moves it and it burns."

"We're going to kill some innocent people that way," said Jacobs.

"Right." Tynan rubbed his face. "Can you rig a timed charge that would give us thirty minutes to get clear?"

"No problem," said Jacobs. "Five minutes."

Tynan crouched then and repeated, "Five minutes."

He watched Jacobs work and then turned, moving so that he could see out toward the airfield where it looked like the circus had just arrived, or someone was selling electric lights. The whole area was ablaze as government officials, Libyan and American, reporters, passengers, and anyone else who could talk his or her way onto the runway, was trying to figure out what had just happened.

"Ready," said Jacobs.

Webster pointed. "He ran in that direction. Off the end of the runway, under a couple of those towers and then angled back."

"You head out there," said Tynan, "and try to find any sign of his passing. Jones, you go get a jeep and drive it over here. Jacobs and I will move so that we can support either one of you. Got it?"

"Aye aye, sir."

As Jones started to head toward the Libyan vehicle park, Webster moved toward the approach towers. Tynan moved with Webster, as did Jacobs. As they moved away, Tynan looked back once, at the body of the dead SEAL. He was sorry that there was nothing he could do for the man now. There wouldn't be a proper burial, and his family would only know that he had disappeared, but he had done a good job. He'd been there, when help was needed.

"I'll hoist one in your honor when we get back," said Tynan quietly.

He moved off, after Jacobs who was angling away from Webster and Jones, trying to get to a position between the two of them. Tynan followed, watching, and waiting for the detonation of the termite grenade.

Jacobs stopped as Jones dropped to the sand near the edge of the runway. Attention there was still focused on the passengers and the news media, though a few of the Libyan officers seemed to be staring out, over the sand. No one had yet realized that several more Libyan soldiers were dead in the sand. The confusion still reigned.

"So far, so good," said Tynan, but then wondered if they should just get out. No one was looking for them. Yet.

12

The television news report told her nothing that she wanted to know. The screen was filled with a riot of pictures, few explained, as the cameraman tried to get the best shot and the men and women working in New York didn't know which shot would be the important one. King crouched in front of the television, her hand on the channel selector, flipping from one station to the next, trying to sort it all out.

She got bits of stories, as the reporter shouted into the camera that the hijacking was over. Libyan guards and hijackers were dead and all the attackers had gotten away. There were reports of American sailors and reports of Israeli commandos. No one knew what was happening.

At one point a commentator in the New York studio informed everyone that they were not reporting rumors. "Everything we tell has been confirmed." He then claimed that the Soviets had loaned a crack squad of the Spetsnaz to the Libyans to resolve the situation.

King got up and walked into the bathroom and ran cold water. She splashed it on her face and then looked at herself in the mirror. "He's okay," she told her reflection. "If something had happened, they'd have known that."

She returned to the television where the reporters and commentators were still trying to resolve the situation. They were talking about Americans again, but some of the passengers, interviewed on the runway, and then inside the terminal, claimed that it wasn't the Americans. Those who had earlier believed it were now telling the reporters that they had gotten caught up in the moment. There were no Americans.

Again and again, the reporters were saying the same things. Someone had stormed the plane, the hijackers were dead, as were several Libyan soldiers. The speculation was suddenly the Libyans had attacked, trying to end the ordeal. The important thing, said the reporters on each of the networks, was that none of the passengers were hurt in the assault.

"Damn it," said King, tears in her eyes, "What in the hell is going on?"

Jones stayed in the shadows which was becoming harder to do. It seemed that everyone in Libya was interested in the activity at the airport and that everyone was now trying to get to the airfield. He swung wide, running hunched over, avoiding the growing pools of light.

There was movement in front of him and he dived for cover behind a scrub bush. He rolled right and then froze. One man was talking to another, but they didn't seem excited. A moment later they turned and moved back toward the runway.

With that, Jones was up and moving again. He reached the fence at the edge of the field and stopped, kneeling. In front of him was a line of vehicles with no one around them. Jeeps, trucks and a couple of cars.

Jones moved forward, to the lead jeep. He crouched next to it, looked up over the hood and saw the people on the runway. A great crowd of people talking, shouting, laughing, crying, and giving orders.

Keeping low, he climbed into the driver's seat and leaned down, so that the rear of the seat would cover him, making it hard for someone behind to see him. He studied the jeep, saw that it was modeled after those produced in the United States, and searched for the ignition. The switch was on the right side of the wheel, above the accelerator.

Jones pumped the gas pedal twice, and then used the switch. The engine turned over but didn't catch. He let go, tried it again and then held it. It turned over, the starter grinding, but then caught. He fed it a little gas, heard the engine backfire once and then roar smoothly.

He sat up and shifted into first. Someone yelled at him and he turned to see a man in a khaki uniform running at him. Jones waved as he popped the clutch. The jeep lurched forward, the tires screaming on the dry pavement. He hit the sand then, and threw up a cloud of dust as he rocketed forward.

Glancing over his shoulder, he saw the man standing on the runway, his hands on his hips as he watched Jones drive away. Jones figured the man didn't realize that the jeep was being stolen.

He headed out, into the desert, without the lights, searching for Tynan and the others. As he bounced, hitting ruts and rocks, and wondering how the desert could be so rough, he was laughing. It had been so easy to steal the jeep that it hardly seemed fair.

Webster, still carrying the Dragunov sniper rifle, loped across the sand until he reached the towers that held the approach lights. He stopped near one, crouched and surveyed the sand under it. Before he arrived, he knew that he wouldn't be able to see footprints. The sand was too soft to hold good prints. But he also knew that he'd hit the man once with one of the 7.62 mm rounds. Maybe the shoulder, maybe the arm, maybe the upper chest. Didn't make any difference where because the man would be bleeding and it was the blood that Webster was looking for.

He got down lower, using the light bleeding from the runway where all hell was breaking loose, and searched for the small, black stain. Blood, in low light, looked black. A wet place on the sand where it all should be dry.

There was nothing visible under the tower. He crawled to the right, found nothing and moved on. As he neared the second tower, he spotted it. Nothing much, just a small place next to one of the uprights. It looked as if the terrorist had leaned there and tried to stop the bleeding. He marked the spot with a stick stripped from one of the many scrub bushes that grew in the shadow of approach light towers.

"Got you, you son of a bitch," he said.

He studied the ground, looking for a second smear of blood that would give him a direction. A better feel for which way the terrorist had taken.

He crawled around, but there was no second puddle. Just the first one. It looked as if the man had managed to stop the bleeding.

The tiny walkie-talkie that he carried crackled to life. "Say status."

Webster took the radio out of his pocket, feeling like a fool. Kids back in the States were using the same toy to play their war games.

"Searching," he said.

"Roger."

He moved on, crawling on his hands and knees, the rifle now slung over his shoulder. He wanted to use his penlight, but couldn't take the chance. He moved in an ever expanding circle, farther and farther from the center of the second tower. Just as he was about to give up, he found it. Hardly more than a few drops, but enough. He stuck a stick into the center of the spot so that he would be able to find it again.

Looking back toward the first tower, he figured the angle and crawled away from the airfield and the mess brewing on the runway. He kept moving, glancing right and left. After ten minutes, now out of sight of the jet and the celebrating passengers, he found another, larger pool of blood. The hijacker had apparently soaked the bandage. A few steps later, he found another spot and then another.

He took out his radio and keyed the mike. "I've got it," he radioed.

"Roger. We're coming."

Webster put the radio away and continued on. He was no longer looking for spots of blood. The trail had been straight from the towers.

He climbed a sand dune carefully. He reached the top and took a sighting on the line of sticks that he had erected. Still it was a straight line.

He worked his way across the top of the dune and looked out over a valley. A wide valley that dropped away slowly. He could see a road not far away, only a hundred or a hundred and fifty yards. There was a single car sitting there.

Webster pulled the sniper rifle off his shoulder and used the scope. He focused on the car, saw that it was running and then saw that the hijacker was not far from it.

Using the radio, he said, "Got him."

The voice that came back was Tynan's. "We're on the way with transport."

Webster put the radio aside and sighted on the wounded man. He was closer to the car now, only a few feet from it. A door opened and someone got out, running toward the wounded man. The hijacker stopped moving and got to his feet wavering back and forth. The other shape caught up to him as the man began to topple over.

Webster began to squeeze the trigger. He took up the slack, took a deep breath, exhaled half of it and made the shot. Just as he pulled the trigger, the people stumbled, falling to the sand. The shot passed harmlessly over them, disappearing into the sand on the other side of the road.

Webster peered through the scope again. The people were near the rear of the car and he lost them in the vague, charcoal darkness that surrounded the vehicle.

The shapes never dissolved so that he couldn't make a shot. He didn't want to gun down an innocent, though anyone out there to pick up the terrorist probably wasn't innocent.

There was a rumble behind him and he saw the jeep coming across the desert. He glanced back, saw the lights of the car come on and then saw it pull out, onto the road.

He stood up and waved his arms, catching the attention of the men in the jeep. It turned toward him and he started running toward it.

Tynan saw the jeep come off the airfield. One Libyan stood on the tarmac, seeming to shout, but made no move to stop the jeep. Tynan got to his feet, waved at the jeep. It veered toward him and stopped. Jacobs leaped into the back and Tynan climbed into the passenger's seat.

Tynan pointed and said, "That way."

As Jones shifted into first and stepped on the gas, the radio crackled to life. "Got him."

Tynan keyed his radio said, "We're on the way with transport."

The jeep crossed the open ground. Tynan spotted the sticks that Webster had stuck into the ground. There was a single rifle shot and a moment later, Jacobs said, "There he is. There's Webster."

Jones spun the wheel, shifted and they drove up the sand dune. The engine roared and the tires spun, throwing up rooster tails of sand.

They reached the top of the dune and Webster ran over to them. He pointed at the receding taillights. "That's him. He's in that car."

Webster tossed the rifle into the rear and jumped into the back. As he did, Tynan said, "Go!"

Jones shifted again and drove over the edge of the dune, rushing down toward the road. He slowed, turned, and then pushed the accelerator to the floor. The engine noise increased as did the roar from the wind.

Far in front of them the taillights of the car flashed once but didn't disappear. They hadn't turned, but stayed on the highway.

Tynan turned in the seat and shouted, "You get a good look at the car?"

"No sir," responded Webster. "Didn't notice anything unusual about it."

"Stay with them Jones."

"Aye aye, sir."

Tynan got out his binoculars and tried to focus on the car in the front of them. They were bouncing along. He couldn't get a fix on the taillights and couldn't see anything distinctive.

"Stay with them," he repeated.

Tynan leaned forward then, a hand on the dashboard of the car, holding on. He tried to see something about the car as they rushed to catch it. If they lost it, there was no way that they would be able to find them again.

They gained a little ground. They left the open area of the desert with the dark, low structures that were set back, away from the road, and entered the city. First there wasn't much change. Houses, barns, buildings closer to the road. Stone walls with wooden gates that protected houses, loomed up. There were a few lights. Dim, yellow things that did little to fight the gloom. The road narrowed, and began to twist. A defensive measure by ancient builders. Didn't want to give invaders a wide, straight avenue of attack.

The car they were chasing slowed even more and they pulled within fifty yards of it. Tynan raised a hand and said, "Not too close yet."

"We could take them out here," said Jacobs, leaning forward, a hand on Tynan's shoulder. "Take them where it would be easy and there are no witnesses."

"I want to find the den," said Tynan. "Take out a bunch of them in retribution."

"Yeah," said Jones glancing to the right.

The car turned and Tynan said, "Pull to the corner and snuff the lights."

They slowed and crept forward. When they reached the cross street, the terrorist's car was gone.

"Shit. Lost them," snapped Jacobs.

"No," said Tynan. "They've turned in somewhere. They're very close. We just have to find them."

"How?"

Tynan shot a glance into the back. He then turned and looked down the street. It was little more than a dirt track outlined by stone walls. There were no street lights and almost no lights in any of the buildings behind the walls. Weeds grew tall by the walls and there was a dog barking somewhere in the distance.

The air was hot and dry and there was the odor of an open sewer. Not a strong odor, one that was partially masked by rotting garbage.

"All right," said Tynan. "We work our way down the street, peek over the walls until we find our boy. Once he's spotted we regroup and decide the best way to hit the place."

"And then we get out, right?" said Jones.

"And then we get out." Tynan pointed at Jacobs and Webster. "You take the left and Jones and I'll take the right. Any questions?"

"No sir," said Jacobs.

"Okay. When you find them, use the radio. Let's go."

They got out of the jeep. Jacobs and Webster crossed the street and then crouched near the dung colored stone wall. In the dim light, Tynan could see them as dark shapes. It was almost impossible to tell that they were human, but he could see them.

Jones touched his shoulder and said, "Ready, Skipper."

Tynan moved along the wall, staying no more than a foot from it. He came to a large, wooden gate with metal spikes set into the top of it. There were two small, rectangular windows in the gate. Tynan glanced in and saw nothing that would suggest the terrorists were inside. He could see an open area in front of the low building, a shed to one side that looked as if it was about to collapse and a tree next to that. There was no indication that a car had pulled in there.

They moved along, and peeked over the wall. Shards of glass topped it, twinkling in the moonlight. The terrorists weren't there either. The building protected by the wall had burned at some point. It was no more than ruins.

Tynan shot a glance across the street. Jacobs was moving along the base of a stone wall, hunched over, his weapon in his hands. Now he looked human. Webster was missing and then he moved, separating himself from a shadow thrown by a towering weed.

Now Jones moved in front of Tynan. He worked his way along the wall, stopped and then started again. Another dog started barking, but that one was far away too.

As they moved, Tynan realized just how quiet it was. Not the normal sounds that he would associate with a city. No car engines or horns. No music blaring. No electrical hum or the rattle of air conditioning. And no voices, just a lone dog barking and then that too ended. It was as if he was moving through a city of the dead. No one there to make noise.

Now he could hear the sound of Jones' feet on the ground and the rasp of his breathing. Quiet sounds that were suddenly as loud as a jet's turbines. He wanted to tell Jones to shut up and be careful, but knew that it would make too much noise. Jones would have to realize it himself and then try to move more quietly.

Jones stopped moving and peeked into another yard. He then dropped down, crouching, and pointed at the wall.

Tynan stood up and looked over. There was a car parked inside and there were lights on in the house. The windows had been boarded over so that little light could escape, but there was no mistaking it. They had found the terrorist's lair.

Tynan sat down, his back to the wall and took out his radio. He keyed it and was all too aware of the noise it made. A slight rustle of static. Not the high quality, precision instrument that he was used to, but a kid's toy that was more than adequate for the job.

He keyed the mike and whispered. "Found them."

Across the street, Jacobs froze and then turned. He said something to Webster, the light breeze catching the sound of his voice, but not the words. Jacobs pointed and then the two of them crossed the street, moving toward Tynan, in a low, slow lope that didn't make noise.

Both Webster and Jacobs crouched in front of him. Jones retreated and looked at him. Tynan could almost make out the features of their faces in the light from overhead. From inside the building, he could now hear voices. Quiet voices speaking a foreign language.

"What now, Skipper?" asked Jones, his lips inches from Tynan's face, his voice almost impossible to hear even in the silence around them.

"Recon."

"How?"

"Jones, you stay here. Webster, you move to the other side of the gate and hold. Jacobs, you go with him and then over the wall, but into the next yard. I'll do the same here. Take five minutes, see what you can and then come back here. But no more than five minutes. Once we know more about this place, we can hit it."

"It's only an hour or so to sunrise," said Jones.

"Then we'd better hurry. And no mistakes. Anyone gets into trouble, you open fire. That'll warn the rest of us," ordered Tynan.

"Aye aye, Skipper," said Jacobs.

"No innocents get hurt," warned Tynan. "We run into anyone around here and we all get the hell out. The terrorists get a free pass."

"Yes sir," said Jones.

Tynan looked at his watch and held up a hand. "Five minutes. We go over the walls in one minute."

Neither Jacobs nor Webster said a word. They turned and moved out, staying close to the wall. As they moved, Tynan did the same thing. He reached the corner, checked his watch and when a minute had passed, he stood up. Without a glance at anyone, he leaped up, and over the wall.

Retribution had begun.

13

For an instant, Tynan crouched in the dark and surveyed
the ground around him. Sand that led up to a dilapidated
house. The front door looked as if it was falling in and the
windows, though dark, seemed to be open. There were
weeds growing near the house, a large bush stuck in the
corner of the walled courtyard, and a pile of rubble at one
side of the house. There were no signs that any humans
were around.

Tynan moved along the wall, keeping his head down.
He listened to the night sounds. Insects and lizards. And
there were quiet voices coming from the terrorist headquarters next door.

He stopped once and peeked over the wall. The car was
on the other side of the house, the rear end of it barely
visible. There was a porch on the front of the house. Not
much of a porch, more of an awning to keep the sunlight
from shining directly in the front door.

Tynan dropped down and moved farther. When he
peeked, he saw that he was at the side of the house. There
was a single window above him, but that had been boarded
shut. No light escaped around it.

He reached the rear of the property and stood in the
corner of the wall. The rear of the terrorist house had a
huge balcony on it. Louvered wooden doors were spaced
along the back, all of them closed. The railing was made of

sculptured metal. Like the front, there was very little light visible and there was no sound at all. That had to mean the terrorists were in the front which made the problem a little simpler.

The backyard was open with the hulk of a vehicle sitting off in one corner. One man there could cover the back and be protected from all sides.

There was no sign of a guard in the rear. Tynan looked over the rear wall, into an alley loaded with debris, boxes, cans and garbage. There was no sign of anyone back there, though a couple of animals were sniffing at a pile of trash.

Satisfied that all the terrorists were inside the house, Tynan hurried back the way he had come. When he reached the front wall, he hesitated and peeked over the wall a final time. A single door in front, a couple of windows and no other ways in or out. Back covered by one man. They should be able to get in without the terrorists seeing them.

He put his hands up on the wall, splaying his fingers to avoid the broken glass. He hopped, lifting himself, and then shifted his weight so that he could put a foot up. With that, he rolled over the top and dropped down on the other side.

Jones came at him and Tynan held up his hand, stopping him. He leaned back against the wall and took a deep breath. He felt the sweat on his body. It spread across his forehead and dripped.

Jacobs returned a minute later and hurried over to where Tynan waited.

"What'd you see?"

"No sign of guards. Long balcony on the rear and a car shoved into the corner of the wall. Structure on my side of the wall was deserted."

"All right," said Tynan quietly. "Webster, I want you to take a position in the rear behind that car and shoot anyone who comes out on the balcony."

"Anyone?" asked Webster. "Could be an innocent."

Tynan hesitated. He realized his order was the kind that led to atrocities in war. And this wasn't a war. But the wrong decision could put his own men in jeopardy.

"Use your judgment," said Tynan finally, "but don't hesitate if you see a weapon. Anyone in that building is either a terrorist or collaborating with the terrorists."

"Aye aye, sir."

"You'll have five minutes to get into place." He glanced at Jacobs and Jones. "We'll go over the wall and hit the front. All of us into the front door. Silenced pistols to begin, but if we run into trouble, automatic weapons. Jones, you go in with the AK to cover us."

"Aye aye, sir."

"Do we shoot everyone inside the house, Skipper?" asked Jacobs.

"Anyone running at us is hostile and will be shot. Anyone fleeing, let's see what happens. The working assumption is that anyone inside is the enemy."

"How we going to know if we got the leader?" asked Jones.

"Easy. He'll be the one who's wounded. We get him, we get the hell out."

"Skipper, it strikes me that we should do something to let them know who did this."

"No," said Tynan. "They'll just know that American sailors did it. They'll know because of the reports that American sailors saved the passengers. They won't know why, they'll just know it happened."

"Seems a waste," said Jones. "Go to all this trouble to get even and then not tell them who did it."

"When you set out on a mission of revenge, you begin by digging two graves. We'll just get even and then get the hell out. Anything else?"

"The car, Skipper," said Jacobs.

"Good point. Jones, once we're inside the compound you disable it. Punch a hole in the gas tank, flatten the tires, anything that will keep them from using it in a pursuit if that should happen."

"Aye aye."

Tynan looked at the men and asked again, "Anything else anyone can think of?"

Each man shook his head in turn.

"Then let's go," said Tynan. "We'll give you five minutes to get into position, Webster, and then we go."

Webster slung the Dragunov sniper rifle and moved off to the south. He stopped, reached up and climbed to the top of the wall. A moment later he disappeared.

"How we going to do this, Skipper?" asked Jacobs.

"We wait for Webster to get into position and then all three of us go over the wall at once. We get to the front door and then get inside."

Tynan fell silent and watched as the second hand moved slowly. When five minutes passed, he stood up and pointed right and left. Jacobs went one direction and Jones the other. Tynan reached up to the top of the wall and dragged the butt of his weapon across it, shearing off the glass shards. He slung his AK so that it would not be in the way. Glancing at Jacobs who was already scrambling over the top.

Tynan grabbed the top and lifted himself up. He rolled over it and dropped to the sand inside the terrorist compound. As he drew the silenced pistol, he studied the interior a final time. Boarded over windows, a sturdy door and just a little light leaking.

Jones entered the compound then. He slipped to the left and moved along the wall. At the car, he laid down and wiggled under it. Using his knife, he punched a hole up into the tank, twisting the blade to widen it. Gas trickled out until Jones got clear. He opened the gas cap. As he did, the bottom seemed to drop out and the gas poured into the sand.

When he finished, he signaled Jacobs who was

crouched near the wall. Tynan stood up then and ran across the sand, bending at the waist, hurrying. He stopped short of the door and turned, moving so that his back was against the wall. When the other two were in position on either side of the door, Tynan reached out for the knob. He slipped to one knee and tried to turn the knob. Surprisingly, it did.

Tynan hesitated, looking up at Jones. He glanced to the left and Jacobs nodded. Tynan edged forward and pushed on the door. There was just an instant of resistance, and then it began to move with no sound.

Tynan stood and pushed it open. No light showed through, though he could see a dim glow inside. He stood up and stepped forward, putting one foot on the floor. Slowly, he rocked forward, putting his weight on that foot and the floor, waiting for it to creak. When it didn't, he entered the terrorist hideout.

Webster had no trouble climbing over the wall and following the path blazed by Jacobs a few minutes earlier. He hurried along the wall, being careful to make no noise. To the left were the ruins of a house and no sign of life around it. He hurried around it and reached the rear of the compound. First, he glanced over the wall, but there was no movement there.

He climbed to the top of the wall, cut his right hand and his left knee on the glass, but ignored the minor wounds. Watching the balcony and the doors, he dropped to the ground and scrambled to the rear, where the car chassis was decaying.

Moving slowly, he moved around it so that the stone wall was against his back. He settled down, getting comfortable. As he did, he shifted once so that he had a clear view of the balcony. Happy with his position, he set out the sniper rifle so that it was pointed up, at the balcony. Using the sight, he studied the doors but there was nothing interesting about them. Four closed doors that revealed nothing.

He looked at the lower level but there was no light coming from it. The rear was sealed tight. Nothing for him to do but wait for someone to show himself.

He let the rifle rest on the hood of the car and took out his canteen. He drank from it, swallowing the water quickly. His thirst quenched, he set the canteen down, near his right hand where he could grab it again if he wanted it.

"Okay, Skipper," he thought. "Now's the time."

Tynan glanced around quickly, inside the terrorist headquarters. A hallway, short, with a stone floor led to the rear. It branched off at right angles. From the right side came a dim light and voices. From the left there was nothing.

Tynan slipped over, his back against the left wall. In his right hand, he held his silenced pistol, a round chambered so that it was ready to fire. The safety was off.

Jacobs had entered the hallway now. He stood to the right, away from the door so that he wasn't silhouetted in it. He waited for Tynan to move again.

Pointing to the right side of the building, Tynan began moving then. He took a single step and froze. There was a scrape of leather on the stone.

Tynan went to one knee, watching the hallway in front of him. A shadow fell across it and a man appeared. A small man with a black beard wearing white clothing. Around his waist was a pistol belt that looked as if it had been manufactured in the United States.

Tynan didn't hesitate. He aimed at the man's head and pulled the trigger of the twenty-two. The round hit the man in the side of the head. He grunted in surprise, snapping both hands to the side of his head as blood spurted. He stood for a second, turned to look at Tynan, surprise registering on his face.

Before he could scream or shout, Tynan fired a second

time. The man dropped to the floor as if all the strength had suddenly drained from his muscles. He slowly rolled to his back as blood pumped from his head. It pooled around him, almost like a crimson halo.

Tynan leaped forward to the corner of the hallway and peeked around the corner. The hallway was empty. There was a stairway at the end of the hall, leading to the second floor.

Pointing at Jacobs and then the spot where he now crouched, Tynan then moved forward. He put a finger against the throat of the man he'd shot, but there was no pulse. The man had been dead before he'd hit the floor.

Keeping his back against the wall, Tynan moved down the hallway. As he did, the sound of the voices became louder. The tone seemed to be jovial. They still suspected nothing was wrong. Tynan used the noise they were making to cover the sounds of his movement down the hall. He reached the edge of the steps and then turned to where he could barely see Jacobs.

Jacobs moved forward then, passed the body of the dead man. He kept his back to the wall, walking just as Tynan had done a moment before.

As he neared, Tynan put a foot on the first step. He kept his eyes on the top of the stairs, his right shoulder against the wall. He stepped on the edge of the riser, trying to keep the stairs from creaking. Slowly he climbed the stairs, waiting for someone to appear there and shout a warning.

He reached the top and saw that the hallway there was almost the duplicate of the one below him. But here there were doorways that led into rooms. Doors that had light bleeding under the base of them.

Just as he reached the top, one of the doors close to him opened. A woman, dressed in nothing, stepped into the hallway. She called out, as if shouting to a friend, and then turned, looking directly into Tynan's eyes.

Before she could scream, Tynan struck, punching her

on the point of the jaw. She groaned in surprise and fell to the floor and didn't move.

A voice from one of the rooms called to her. There was a moment of silence, and then another, louder shout. Tynan crouched, waiting for the man to appear in the hallway. A second later, one of the doors opened. As the man appeared, he saw Tynan and dived back, inside. Tynan snapped off a shot that buried itself in the door jamb.

There was another loud shout, answered by several men. Tynan whirled and yelled down at Jacobs, "That's torn it. They know we're here."

As he shouted, there was a burst of fire from the lower level as Jones shot at someone. His voice drifted up. "They've spotted us, Skipper."

Jacobs ran up the stairs and crouched, his AK out, aimed down the hall. When a door opened, he fired, riddling it, but hit no one.

"Now what?"

"Let's get the hell out of the open."

Tynan leaped over the unconscious body of the naked woman. He kicked at the door. When it flew open, he dived through, rolling once and coming up. There was a flash of movement to his right and he whirled, firing. The bullets shattered a mirror hanging on the wall.

Noise erupted everywhere. People were shouting. There were single shots and bursts from automatic weapons. Tynan cleared the room and crawled back to the door just as Jacobs leaped in.

"Fucked that up," he said.

Tynan yanked the door so that it was wide open. He crawled forward and peeked into the hallway. The lights that had been glowing suddenly went out and a quiet hum that he hadn't noticed until then died.

"Generator," he said.

"Skipper," shouted Jones from the lower floor.

"Shit," said Tynan. Jones was down there by himself.

There was nothing he could do for him. "Get out," shouted Tynan. Then he pulled out the small walkie-talkie and repeated the order.

"How you want to handle this?" asked Jacobs.

"They're at the same disadvantage we are. Can't see shit. Let's move on them."

"They know the house," said Jacobs.

"True. They also know that time is on their side. No incentive to make a move. Let's attack and then get out."

A male voice called out something. It sounded like a question, but Tynan didn't know. He understood nothing of the language.

Jacobs crawled forward, snaked an arm out into the hallway and pulled the woman in, out of the line of fire. He checked her pulse and then ignored her.

"Let's go," said Tynan. Without waiting, he began to crawl along the floor, keeping his head and butt down. He held his AK by the pistol grip in his right hand. Staying near the wall, he re-entered the hallway. It was still dark, but not pitch black. He could see shapes. A table, the charcoal of a window at the far end of the hallway.

The ideal way to clear the rooms was to roll a grenade into each one and follow it with a burst of automatic weapons fire. He hesitated, afraid of innocent people getting caught in the firefight, but then decided that there were no innocents in the building.

When he reached the first door, he pushed on it. It gave a fraction so he pulled a grenade. He yanked the pin free, shoved on the door and rolled the grenade into the room. As he did, he fell face down, covering his eyes to protect his night vision from the flash.

There was a hot blast of air as the grenade exploded. Shrapnel whistled through the air and cut into the walls. There was a single scream of anguish that was cut off abruptly. Tynan moved then, diving into the room. As he rolled to the right, he heard the quiet crying of a wounded man. A low, whimpering that said the man was badly hurt, probably dying.

In the dark, Tynan could see nothing. He turned toward the sound. The man, knowing there was someone in the room with him, called out, hesitated and fired a pistol. In the strobe of the muzzle flash, Tynan saw the wounded man sitting on the floor, blood covering his head and chest. Tynan fired into that area, heard the man hit and the body fall.

"Skipper?"

"Go."

"Next room."

Tynan crawled to the door. It wasn't going to work. There wasn't enough time and he didn't have enough people to clear the headquarters. They'd get trapped and eliminated. The smart move was to get out. They'd already won a partial victory. They'd entered the building and killed a couple of the enemy terrorists. It would have to be enough.

"Let's get out," called Tynan.

As he spoke, another grenade detonated. There was a burst of machine gun fire in response. Tynan saw a tracer flash down the hall to bury itself in the wall. The machine gun fell silent and then opened fire again. The gunner was holding the trigger down, spraying the hallway, hoping to hit someone by accident. Until he stopped shooting, Tynan was trapped in the room.

An AK joined the din. Bullets were slamming into the walls, ripping them apart. There was shouting as the terrorists tried to coordinate their activity. Tynan knew that it was all over. With the element of surprise gone, he'd have to retreat.

"Pull back," he shouted.

"Trapped," said Jacobs.

"Give me cover fire."

"You got it."

Another weapon joined in the firing. As it did, Tynan

crawled forward and tried to look into the hallway. He could see the muzzle flashes from the machine gun, looking like the strobe of a camera gone berserk. But he couldn't see where the machine gun was hidden. Again he pulled a grenade, jerked the pin free and then watched as the tracers rocked back and forth across the hall. When he had the rhythm, he rocked out as the tracers moved away from him, threw the grenade at the center of the muzzle flash and dropped to the floor.

An instant later the grenade exploded. There was a scream as the machine gun fell silent.

"Now," shouted Tynan.

With that, he was up and moving. Staying low, close to the wall, he ran for the steps. As he reached them, he turned and dropped down, letting the floor protect him. A shape came at him and Tynan shouted, "ID."

"Christ, it's me."

Tynan popped up and fired a quick burst to protect Jacobs. As the big man hit the steps, Tynan said, "Go! Go!"

For a moment, it had seemed that everything would be fine. There was no sound from anywhere in the house, except the voices that had been talking from the moment they had entered. Jones had followed Tynan in and then had covered the hallway as the Skipper and Jacobs had gone down the hall to climb the stairs.

A few minutes after they disappeared, a door at the other end of the hall opened. A square of light fell across the hall and someone began walking toward him. He stopped, saw the man lying on the floor and started to shout. Jones knew that there was nothing he could do. He pointed his weapon and squeezed the trigger. The rounds took the man in the stomach, lifted him and threw him to the floor.

As that happened, firing broke out above him. There

was shouting and shooting and then the explosion of a grenade. Jones backed up, toward the front door. He reached it, and stopped, watching the hallway, waiting for the terrorists to show themselves.

Jones wasn't sure what to do then. He needed to protect Tynan and Jacobs who were above him. He advanced to the end of the hallway and glanced right and left. There was no one anywhere to be seen.

He crouched, watching the bottom of the steps. He listened to the firefight developing above him. There was a temptation to run up the stairs to help, but that wasn't his job. Protecting the rear was it. If he left his post, then Tynan and Jacobs could be surprised.

Then, to the left he heard a noise. Turning, he saw a door close and then open. One man leaped out, rolled and opened fire with a pistol. Rounds snapped through the air. Jones jumped to the rear, flattening himself against the floor and lying up against the wall.

As he moved, two more men came running down the hallway, firing as they ran. Jones pulled the trigger of his weapon. It kicked back, against his shoulder. The rounds hit the running men about knee high and spilled them to the floor. As they fell, they dropped their weapons. One man rolled to his back, his hands wrapped around his thigh as blood poured from the wound. The other screamed and tried to crawl to cover, but a bullet shattered his forehead, dropping him to the floor.

Now the last man scrambled to the rear, trying to reach cover. Jones slipped forward, aimed and fired. The man collapsed to the floor as his weapon skidded away from his hand.

Jones retreated, ripped the magazine from his weapon and replaced it. There were a few rounds left in the banana clip, but Jones wanted a fully loaded one in case more of the terrorists burst into the hallway.

With his fully loaded AK, he crawled forward to guard

the hall. In the dim light, he could see smoke and dust hanging in the air. He could taste and smell and feel it. There were now shadows and shapes dancing in the smoke caused by the light and the dust. He prayed that Tynan and Jacobs would get the hell out of there so that they could clear the building.

Outside, Webster could hear everything that happened inside. He heard the shouting and the shooting and the grenades exploding. He could see the flashes of light as the grenades detonated into fountains of orange yellow sparks and he could see the tracers burning through the night. Flashes from the muzzles of the weapons strobed. Shapes appeared and vanished in quick succession.

Through it all, Webster could only sit behind the hulk of the car, snug up against the stone of the wall's corner, and wait. One set of doors on the balcony burst open, but no one came out. A shape moved behind the door, but Webster had no idea who it was. He wasn't going to fire into the darkness at any unidentified shape. Not when three of his own men were inside the house.

As the firing inside continued, Webster felt his stomach grow cold and flip over. He had missed the fight on the jet because he was the sniper and now he was missing the fight in the house because he was the sniper. His fellows were in danger, maybe fighting for their lives, and he sat in a makeshift bunker and waited for a chance to make one, maybe two shots. No one knew he was there. He was safe, and that irritated him.

He shifted once, thinking about rushing the back door of the house, but then didn't move. His job was to stay right where he was, waiting in case a few of the terrorists tried to escape to the rear. The moment he came out of hiding, the terrorists would appear to exploit his mistake. No matter how badly he wanted to run into the fight, how badly his stomach churned and how rapid his breathing became, he had to sit right where he was. He clenched his teeth and doubled his fists as the adrenaline pumped through him making it nearly impossible to sit still. And he waited.

There were more explosions inside the house but the firing tapered slightly. The other doors flew open, but still no one appeared there. A phantom flashed past and vanished into the darkness inside.

Then there was more movement. A single shape appeared, moved out onto the balcony, but before Webster could see it well, it dropped down, hiding behind the iron railing. Webster swung the barrel of the Dragunov around and peered through the three power scope mounted on the top.

The shadows resolved themselves slightly. He could see a potted plant by the doors. A bench near the railing and the kneeling shape of one of the terrorists. Webster thought about firing and then decided to wait to see what would happen.

A second person came out the door. A man wearing khaki pants and carrying an AK-47. He was bare chested with a spot of white on his shoulder. A bandage that had been taped there.

Webster suddenly knew that he was looking at the man who had escaped from the airport. He put the sight-post of the scope in the center of the man's chest, but before he could shoot, the man dropped to his knees behind the railing, next to the first person there.

The first person stood then and climbed up over the rail to drop to the ground. Webster could see that it was a woman. Long black hair, khaki shirt and cut off pants. A short, slender woman. She too had a weapon, but Webster ignored her. She wasn't the target.

She crouched and dropped to the ground. She rolled to her shoulder and then jumped up. She turned and looked back, at the balcony.

As she did, the terrorist stood and slowly, carefully

climbed over the railing. As he did, he was motionless for an instant as he straddled the railing, almost as if trying to retain his balance. That was what Webster had been waiting for. With the sight post center on the man's chest, he pulled the trigger as the terrorist stopped moving.

The round caught the man dead center and flipped him back, over the rail. His weapon went sailing into the air as he tossed it away in reflex. He disappeared from sight, falling to the balcony deck.

As he did, the woman whirled and fired with her weapon, but the rounds were high and wide. She didn't know where the shot had come from. She stood there, firing from the hip, spraying the bullets like water from a garden hose. When the weapon was empty, the bolt locked back, she screamed and turned. As she tossed the AK to the sand at her feet, she scrambled forward, trying to climb back up onto the balcony.

Webster let her go, his job finished.

14

"Jones," shouted Tynan. "We're coming down."

"Got you covered, Skipper."

Jacobs was halfway down the stairs. He had stopped and turned, facing the top. There was firing from some of the rooms up there and there were flames and smoke pouring from others. The terrorists were shouting.

Tynan fired a burst into the closed door at the far end of the hallway and then jumped clear. He landed on the floor on his belly and scrambled to the top of the steps, sliding over. He spun around facing the hallway and fired another burst.

Glancing over his shoulder, he saw Jacobs moving down. "Go!" he shouted.

As Jacobs reached the bottom, Tynan emptied his weapon into the wall and door about halfway down the hall. He hit the release and jerked the banana clip free. Tossing it aside, he grabbed another, slamming it home. Working the bolt, he started down the steps. When he reached the bottom, he whirled.

A man had appeared at the top of the stairs, aiming his AK down at Tynan. Tynan fired from the hip, holding the trigger down. The rounds cut the man's feet out from under him, dropping him. Two more rounds hit him in the back as he fell. He lost his weapon as he tumbled down the stairs, smearing them with blood.

"Go!" Tynan urged Jacobs.

The big man crawled around so that he could see down the ground floor. Smoke and dust obscured his view. There were lumps lying on the floor. Men killed by Tynan and Jones lay where they had fallen.

A shape loomed up, an AK held in one hand. "Jones?"

The man didn't answer but Jones did, from behind him. "I'm here."

Jacobs opened fire and the enemy fell to the floor. As he did, Jacobs was on his feet. "I'm coming toward you."

"Come on."

Jacobs moved and Tynan stood up. Above him there was shouting and shooting. Wood smoke was boiling down the stairs, filling the house. Tynan fired a burst up the stairs at the shadows and then whirled.

Jacobs was running through the dust and smoke. Tynan followed him, almost catching him. He leaped around the corner that led to the front door.

"Go," Tynan yelled at Jones.

The younger man got to his feet and retreated. He kicked the door open and jumped out, into the fresh air of the night. Tynan waved at Jacobs who took off out the door and ran to the gate leading into the street. Tynan hesitated, but there was no sign of a pursuit. He spun and ran out the door, diving to the sand on one side of it. As he did, Jones ran after Jacobs.

Jacobs fired a burst into the gate. He raised a foot and kicked. The door swung open and Jacobs leaped through, turned and aimed back at the house.

When the gate opened, Tynan scrambled to his feet. He glanced at the front of the house. Smoke was boiling out the windows of the second floor. Flames danced. There was shouting and screaming, but no one appeared. Tynan ran back, toward the gate.

As soon as he was clear, he fell back against the wall. He pulled out his walkie-talkie and said, "Get clear."

There was a moment's hesitation and then a quiet, "Roger."

"Now what?" asked Jones.

"We get the fuck out of here," said Tynan grinning. "Jones, get to the jeep and get it started."

"Aye aye, sir."

As Jones moved there was a burst of fire from the rear of the compound. Jones dived to the ground. Tynan tried to peek around the gate as Jacobs crouched.

The radio crackled. "I'm pinned down. Firing from the house to the south."

Jacobs looked at Tynan and said, "I wondered where all those people were coming from."

"Meaning?"

"They probably have tunnels to the main house from those supposedly deserted houses on either side."

Tynan nodded and then looked at Jones. "Get to the jeep and get it started. Get back here to pick us up."

"Aye."

There were three well spaced shots then. Tynan knew that it was Webster using his rifle to stop the terrorists. Tynan keyed the mike on his small radio and said, "We'll give you covering fire."

"Roger."

Jacobs shifted farther to the south, peeked over the wall and dropped down again. "Can't see anyone," he whispered.

Tynan used the radio. "Can you stay on this side of the wall and move along it?"

"Maybe."

"When you hear the firing, take off."

"Roger."

Tynan set the radio down and picked up his weapon. He glanced over the wall at the headquarters they had assaulted. Flames were now coming from parts of the roof, lighting the clouds of smoke curling upward. The sky was

beginning to lighten as the sun came up. But there was no
sign of life there.

Tynan nodded at Jacobs and said, "On three. One. Two.
Three."

As he spoke, he opened fire, raking the windows in the
headquarters. He saw a few of the rounds smash through
the wood that had blocked the windows. Flames ate their
way through and part of the roof fell in. The courtyard
brightened in the flickering of the fire.

Jacobs was shooting and then, suddenly ducked. Firing
erupted from the house in the next courtyard. Tynan turned
his attention on one of the windows, raking it with bullets.
He aimed into the muzzle flashes. That weapon fell silent,
but others began to shoot.

Then, from the burning headquarters, a machine gun
opened up. The heavy slugs slammed into the wall, shat-
tering part of it. Stone and dust flew. Tynan dropped to the
ground as the machine gun raked the top of the wall.

"Can't make it," said Webster.

"Can you climb over the rear wall?"

"Possibly."

"Do that and then run up the alley toward the street.
We'll pick you up there."

"Roger."

Webster collapsed the antenna of the Radio Shack walkie-talkie and stuffed it into his pocket. He picked up his
canteen and drank the rest of the water from it. There was
firing around him, but none of it directed at him. Firing
from the house to the south, the bullets hitting the wall in
front. Firing from the burning upper floor of the headquarters house, aimed at Tynan and Jacobs in the front.

In the rear, on the balcony, there was no movement. Not
since he'd dropped the terrorist and the woman had
climbed back up. She had dragged the body into the house.

Webster shifted around so that he was kneeling behind

the car. The smart thing would be to jump to the front fender that was up against the rear wall and leap over to the alley behind. Two seconds for the enemy to get off a shot. Not enough time unless someone was very lucky.

He slung his sniper rifle, pulling the sling tight so that it would be held against his back. He glanced to the burning house, saw the roof fall in and a cloud of sparks roll skyward slowly.

As that happened, Webster moved. It was an instinctive thing. Everyone would be watching the fire at that moment. He had the time to get over the wall. He stood, put his hands on the fender and jumped. One foot slipped and he banged his knee, but it didn't stop him. He put his hands on the top of the wall, forgetting about the glass. He shifted his weight and leaped, swinging his feet up and over the top of the wall. The glass cut into his hands as he pivoted.

But then he was on the ground on the farside of the wall. He crouched there, both hands on the sand. He heard firing erupt and heard the bullets smash into the wall protecting him, a couple of them whining off the top. Too little too late.

He unslung his rifle, just in case. Sitting down then, he pulled out the radio and said, "I'm clear. Heading down the alley."

"Roger," came Tynan's voice. "Meet you at the northern end."

"That's got it," said Tynan.

Jacobs ducked and reloaded. "Then we can get the fuck out of here?"

"Now," said Tynan. He popped up and emptied the magazine into the house.

As he did, Jacobs, ducking low, ran toward him, in front of the open gate. Just as he passed it, the machine gun opened fire again, but the rounds were high. They slammed into the closed portion of the gate or into the empty street. Jacobs dived for cover like a base runner trying to beat the throw from the plate.

Tynan reloaded and fired again. He glanced down at Jacobs and yelled, "Go!"

But before the man could get to his feet, the jeep roared around the corner coming at them. With the sun coming up, the blackness that wrapped the street was suddenly a charcoal. The shape of the jeep and the driver were obvious. The machine gunner in the burning building turned his attention on the jeep. Tracers flashed by it and bullets ricocheted from the street.

And then the front of the building collapsed, spilling the upper floor into the sand. The machine gun stopped firing and the man screamed as the flaming debris engulfed him. He staggered to his feet, running at the open gate. Tynan fired once and the man fell, turning into a flaming, burning pile of dead meat.

Jacobs ran toward the jeep as Jones stopped it and spun the wheel before giving it gas. The rear fishtailed, whipping around so that the jeep was facing the way it had come.

Tynan put a final burst into the headquarters and then turned. He ran forward and jumped into the rear. Over the noise of the firing, the popping and crackling of the flames, the screaming and shouting of the terrorists, he yelled, "Let's get going."

Jones ground the gears and popped the clutch. The jeep lurched forward. Tynan rolled up against the rear of the seats as Jones tried to get them clear.

"To the right," ordered Tynan. "We've got to pick up Webster."

Jones hit the brakes at the cross street and turned. He hit the accelerator and then the brake, sliding to a halt. Webster, who had been crouching in the shadows at the corner, leaped forward. He scrambled into the rear of the jeep.

"Glad to see you all," he said.

Jones didn't wait for instructions. He floored the accelerator again, spinning the tires. As they rocketed away Tynan turned and looked to the rear. He could see the glow of the fire in the clouds of smoke billowing higher and higher. The sky was a brighter gray now, outlining the smoke of the fire.

But there seemed to be no sign of a pursuit. The street around them remained free of traffic and nothing appeared behind them.

"Think we're clear, Skipper," said Jacobs.

"Everyone all right?" asked Tynan.

"I cut my hands," said Webster. He held them up, but it was too dark to see much yet.

"We got a first aid kit somewhere?" asked Tynan.

Jacobs handed it back to him. As he opened it, he said, "I don't think we got the leader."

Webster shook his head. "No sir. I got him trying to come out the back."

Jacobs spun and asked, "You sure?"

Tynan took hold of one of Webster's hands and asked, "What the hell you'd do?"

"Forgot about the glass." As Tynan worked to bandage his wounds, he told Jacobs, "I'm not sure. I did get one of them coming out the back who seemed to have on a bandage. I assume that he's the one that I shot at the airfield."

"Skipper, where should I be going?"

"Turn to the south and then back into the center of the city. We'll find the American embassy and give them the story about having our passports stolen."

"What about the jeep?"

"Just park it somewhere and let the locals worry about it."

Jacobs interrupted and asked again, "What about the terrorist leader?"

Webster shrugged. "I think I got him."

Tynan took over. "Doesn't matter now. Jones, let's head toward the embassy. We'd better make the arrangements to get out of here before there is too much heat over the raid."

Jones glanced over his shoulder. "You think anyone will suspect us?"

"No," said Tynan. "They'll think it was the Israeli Mossad. Our government will be pissed at us because we lost our passports but that's all that will happen."

"How long do you think it will take to get the paperwork done?"

Tynan hesitated before answering. He thought about the fact there was no record of them leaving the United States, but then such records could get lost. They were all on leave so travel was not against regulations. The American relationship with Libya wasn't the best, but there were no restrictions on travel to Libya.

Jones turned and they entered the heart of the city. Not the rundown, dilapidated area that he had expected, but a modern city with high rise buildings and glass and steel skyscrapers.

"Well, Skipper?"

Tynan shrugged. Five days, at the most.

15

It took more than five days. As Tynan had suspected, the American authorities were less than thrilled with the arrival of four American sailors who had no passports. The military ID cards, fingerprints and military records established who the Americans were, but not how they had gotten into Libya. With rumors that American sailors had freed the passengers on the hijacked plane running wild, the embassy, under orders from Washington, wanted to do as little as possible to stir up trouble. They moved quietly to get Tynan and his men out of Libya before the media or the Libyans connected them to the raid on the hijacked jet.

Tynan had to sit in the office of the Naval attaché and listen to lectures about his failure to maintain discipline for his men, his poor example to his men, and his failure to use good judgment. Interestingly, the Naval attaché never asked if Tynan had been involved in the raid on the hijacked plane. Again, no one wanted to ask a question to which they didn't want the answer. Everyone pretended that no one had any idea that Tynan and the four men might know something.

Tynan, on the other hand, asked some questions about the hijacking. The local CIA operative, learning that Tynan was a SEAL, began a friendship with him. Through that, Tynan learned that everyone the CIA had identified as involved in the hijacking had either been killed on the aircraft or in a raid on their headquarters an hour or so later. The terrorist leader, a man wounded on the airplane, was found badly burned, lying in the sand behind the ruined headquarters.

"Breaks my heart," said the CIA man sarcastically. "Someone sneaked in there in the middle of the night and shot him as he tried to escape. A real pity."

Tynan, sitting opposite his desk, staring out the window, asked, "Anyone know who did it?"

"The current thought is the Mossad. There were a number of Israelis on the plane. Mossad freed them all and then slipped away to save the Israeli government the embarrassment of having to explain why its agents attacked without coordinating with the Libyans."

"You believe that?" asked Tynan.

"I believe what I'm told to believe and right now our government wants to believe it was the Mossad very badly."

"Well," said Tynan. "It sounds like the kind of renegade action the Israelis favor."

The CIA man stared hard at Tynan and grinned. "It does, doesn't it."

Finally, with a reprimand from the Naval attaché, Tynan and the men were put on a military plane and flown to Germany. It was the first military flight they could be put on and the ambassador wanted them out of Libya before anyone asked some very embarrassing questions about them. In Germany, they were put on another plane bound for Washington. At Andrews Air Force Base, they were met by a caravan of Naval officers who put them into cars and took them to the Pentagon for a long, involved interrogation.

Tynan was unworried about it because he knew how it would work. They would shout, shine bright lights into their eyes as they tried to get someone to change the story. The only problem was that Tynan and the men had had a week to rehearse their story among themselves. No one was going to change his story because someone shouted at him or threatened him.

So he endured the interrogation that was only half-hearted. Everyone around gave the impression that he hoped Tynan had done something about the hijacking. Almost to a man, the Navy wanted to believe that four sailors had stormed an aircraft surrounded by Libyan soldiers, killed the terrorists and freed the passengers. So they didn't try very hard to break the story and when they failed, they gave up easily.

Tynan was escorted upstairs and taken into the office of the chief of Naval Operations. Tynan stood in the huge outer office where two secretaries and a military aide worked and waited for the CNO to condescend to see him.

As he stood there, envisioning an audience with the CNO, he speculated about the nature of the discussion. Would it be a thinly veiled approval of the action or would it be a recommendation for a court martial?

In the end, it turned out to be nothing so dramatic. He was escorted into the office of the CNO's chief aide, told to sit down and then chewed out. The man stood behind his desk and shouted that Tynan had endangered talks, international relations, the United Nations and the free world. Men could no longer mount unauthorized expeditions to foreign lands and engage in any form of diplomacy, even if that diplomacy was in the form of a military action. It was unconstitutional and it was illegal.

"But I was on vacation," protested Tynan. "My passport was stolen."

The aide shook his head, screamed for another five minutes and then dropped into his seat. "A note of this incident is going to be made for your service jacket."

Tynan didn't know whether to applaud or to protest. If all he had done was lose a passport, a notation shouldn't be made. But then, almost everyone who read it would suspect the real story and that could help him. There was a tacit approval of the operation that ran through the entire Navy. Everyone dreamed of the opportunity to do just what Tynan and his men had already done.

In the end, he said simply, "Yes sir."

He left the office and found his way to a telephone on the ground floor of the Pentagon, near one of the main entrances. He stood in the booth, a dime in his hand and then wondered if he should make the phone call. King had not been thrilled with the idea that he was going to Libya to kill the hijackers. She had been less than thrilled with the idea that he was going to extract retribution without waiting for due process.

But then, King said she understood. She would have to. He dropped the dime and called the hotel where they had been staying when he left eight days earlier.

When he was put through to the room and she picked up the phone, he could think of nothing to say, other than a simple, "Hello."

"Mark?"

"The very same."

Her voice cooled and she asked, "Where in the hell are you now?"

"Washington," he said.

"How nice for you. There a reason you called? Finally."

"I was hoping that we could have dinner tonight." He grinned at the reflection of his face in the glass, realizing that she was playing a game with him.

"Dinner?" she said. "I don't know. After not hearing from you for a week, I might have made other plans."

"You know," said Tynan, "that it was impossible for me to call. The telephone systems in Libya aren't the best."

"A cable," said King.

"Also impossible," said Tynan, thinking of the trouble that he had been in while in Libya. The last thing he wanted to do was call attention to her.

"Well dinner tonight might be impossible."

"Anywhere you'd care to go, except Kentucky Fried Chicken."

She laughed at that and then asked, "Are you okay?"

"I'm fine. Lost my passport in Libya," he said, telling her the cover story, "but I managed to convince the embassy that I'm an American. Been back about seven hours."

"And didn't call?"

"Navy had a few questions they wanted answered before I had the chance to make any phone calls."

She weakened then and asked, "How soon can you get over here, Mark?"

"As fast as it takes me to get off the phone and find a taxi."

There was a moment of silence and she said, "Stop wasting time."

Tynan said, "Understood." He hung up and ran out the door in search of a cab. He made it to the hotel in record time.

She was waiting in the lobby.

THE WORLD'S MOST RUTHLESS FIGHTING UNIT, TAKING THE ART OF WARFARE TO THE LIMIT — AND BEYOND!

SEALS #1: AMBUSH!	75189-5/$2.95US/$3.95Can
SEALS #2: BLACKBIRD	75190-9/$2.50US/$3.50Can
SEALS #3: RESCUE!	75191-7/$2.50US/$3.50Can
SEALS #4: TARGET!	75193-3/$2.95US/$3.95Can
SEALS #5: BREAKOUT!	75194-1/$2.95US/$3.95Can
SEALS #6: DESERT RAID	75195-X/$2.95US/$3.95Can
SEALS #7: RECON	75529-7/$2.95US/$3.95Can
SEALS #8: INFILTRATE!	75530-0/$2.95US/$3.95Can
SEALS #9: ASSAULT!	75532-7/$2.95US/$3.95Can
SEALS #10: SNIPER	75533-5/$2.95US/$3.95Can

and coming soon from Avon Books

SEALS #11: ATTACK!	75582-3/$2.95US/$3.95Can
SEALS #12: STRONGHOLD	
	75583-1/$2.95US/$3.95Can

FROM PERSONAL JOURNALS TO BLACKLY HUMOROUS ACCOUNTS

VIETNAM

DISPATCHES, Michael Herr

01976-0/$4.50 US/$5.95 Can

"I believe it may be the best personal journal about war, any war, that any writer has ever accomplished."
—Robert Stone, *Chicago Tribune*

A WORLD OF HURT, Bo Hathaway

69567-7/$3.50 US/$4.50 Can

"War through the eyes of two young soldiers...a painful experience, and an ultimately exhilarating one."
—*Philadelphia Inquirer*

NO BUGLES, NO DRUMS, Charles Durden

69260-0/$3.50 US/$4.50 Can

"The funniest, ghastliest military scenes put to paper since Joseph Heller wrote *Catch-22*"
—*Newsweek*

AMERICAN BOYS, Steven Phillip Smith

67934-5/$4.50 US/$5.95 Can

"The best novel I've come across on the war in Vietnam"
—Norman Mailer

COOKS AND BAKERS, Robert A. Anderson

79590-6/$2.95

"A tough-minded unblinking report from hell"
—*Penthouse*